A Legend Untold

A Legend Untold is a work of fiction. Characters, places, names and events are either the product of the author's imagination or are used fictitiously. Any resemblance to actual persons, either living or dead, places or events is entirely coincidental.

ACKNOWLEDGMENTS

My grateful appreciation to:

'Papaw' Richard Day. This isn't quite where we expected to go with this project, but it all started with you. Thanks for all your support and encouragement.

Jim and Evie Walls. Thanks for applying your editing skills, but, even more, for your tutelage and your friendship.

John 'Santee' Scott. Thanks for helping me stay on the correct historical path and for your kind words of encouragement.

Keelie Jones. Thanks for the cover art and all your help in getting this book published. It would never have been accomplished without you. Even more, thanks for being the best daughter a father could hope for.

Most of all, God. Thank You for whatever aptitude for writing You may have bestowed upon me. It has enriched my life beyond my expectations.

Book 1

A Reluctant Legend

PROLOGUE

"Like I was sayin'," the old man continued, "every now an' then, a boy is born to a legend, whether he wants it or not. An' some legends never get told. Now, you take the untold legend of Colton Bonner..."

This is the story the old man told to me that day.

CHAPTER 1

Life in the nineteenth century American West was hard, and so it was for Colton Bonner. Born in Kentucky, he came west with his mother and father in search of opportunity. His father was killed in an accident during their journey, forcing Colton to become "the man of the family" at the age of fourteen. Trouble seemed to become a way of life for him from that point on.

He and his mother found a good location in Kansas to homestead and they began farming. It was hard work, but Colton applied himself diligently, learning to farm, and to hunt as well. Before long, he developed not only the strength of a more mature man, but also his marksman's eye and his understanding of the trials and challenges that life often brings.

That understanding, unfortunately, was increased the next year. Their spring turned bad and his mother died of fever from the brackish water, leaving Colton on his own at fifteen. The War for Southern Independence had ended not too long before and many former soldiers, especially from

3

the South, were drifting west to start a new life in a wide open land. That sounded to Colton like a good opportunity for him to put his bad memories behind him, so he sold the farm and headed west.

Along the way, he quickly found that a lot of the wandering men he ran across, both on the trail and in the many little towns springing up, tended to settle their differences with guns, especially when whiskey was involved. And whiskey always seemed to be involved. It was even more plentiful in these new towns than wanderers and former soldiers. He realized he would need to become as proficient with a pistol as he was with his rifle.

As he traveled west, Colton would stop at deserted areas and practice with the old Colt revolver that had been his father's. He could see that, not only would marksmanship be essential, but speed would be a great advantage as well. He knew he would need a good holster and a good supply of ammunition for practice, and he also planned to trade his old muzzle-loading rifle for one of those Henry repeaters the first chance he had. He had heard former soldiers saying you could load it on Sunday and shoot it all week. All this would use up a lot of the money he had gotten from the sale of the farm, so he needed to be thinking about earning some more. The idea of cattle soon came to his attention.

After the war, many Southern soldiers found that stray cattle, which had migrated up from Mexico over the decades, had been busy multiplying in the brushes of southern Texas, New Mexico and Arizona. They were unbranded and were available to anyone who wanted to round them up and drive them to a rail head for shipment to eastern markets. Beef was also needed to feed the railroad crews working their way west, and needed further west and north by prospectors in the gold camps and boomtowns.

All this meant that large numbers of cattle were beginning to be driven up out of the border states, and men were needed to do the driving. Colton figured that would be a good way to earn some money, while making his way west as well. He determined to try to hire on to the first cattle drive he found, and he found it around a campfire south of Ellsworth, Kansas.

CHAPTER 2

"I'm lookin' for a job," Colton said to the men eating around the campfire.

They all looked him over and didn't seem to be at all impressed by this thin young boy who, indeed, looked fresh off the farm. One man finally spoke up. "I don't know about the job, but I never turn a man away from the fire hungry."

"Thank you, sir, but I'm not one to take charity. I'd rather work for it, if there's a job available."

"It ain't charity, son," said the man, "it's survival. This is a hard land an' it's a sorry man that won't help a fella. You ever punch cattle?"

"No, sir, but I'm no stranger to hard work."

"Ever eat dust all day behind a herd?"

"No, sir, but I've eat it all day behind a plow."

"Ever spent sixteen hours in a saddle an' got by on four hours sleep a night? An' that's on the nights you ain't ridin' night herd."

"No, sir, but I'll get used to it if I have to."

"What's your name, son?"

"Colton Bonner, sir."

The man sized the boy up for just a moment, then said, "Well, 'Colton Bonner Sir,' I'm Hank Benson, your new boss. Eat up, you'll need it."

A couple of weeks later, they were making good progress, going fast enough to reach Ellsworth during the height of the market, yet slow enough not to take any weight off the cattle. "It ain't that much further to Ellsworth," Hank told Colton. "We'll be sellin' this herd there an' payin' the boys off, then anybody that wants to can go back to Texas with me. If you want to keep goin' west, though, there's other trails further west where you might find another herd to hire onto."

Colton hadn't minded the long hours and the dust as much as he had feared at first. "That's prob'ly what I'll do, Mr. Benson. I appreciate you takin' me on, though."

"You've earned yer keep. Yer a hard worker an' a fast learner. Tell yer next trail boss I said so."

Colton beamed and said, "Thank you, sir."

At Ellsworth, the trail crew was paid off and Colton knew he needed to use his pay wisely. His first wise decision was to stay away from the saloons, gambling halls and the women. It wasn't that difficult. Although he found he didn't dislike whiskey, he hadn't developed the taste for it that most of the others had. Gambling looked to him like a sucker's game, unless you could cheat without getting caught, and women hadn't yet been so tempting to him that he couldn't resist their advances.

No, he had more important ways in mind to spend his money. His first priority was to get a good holster. He found a saddle shop with some holsters in the window and went in to look around. He saw some nice holsters, but not like what he had in mind. He had noticed some men who carried their guns crossdraw style, in front of the left hip but turned to be drawn with the right hand. This made a lot of sense, seeming to afford a shorter, continuous motion for getting the gun into action. He asked about the prices of the holsters he saw and decided that he needed to get a bit creative with his finances if he wanted to have enough money to get a new repeating rifle, and get him into Colorado to the next cattle trail.

He asked the proprietor if business was good. "Got more'n I can handle, what with a bunch of fresh-paid cowhands needin' to replace some wore-out rigs."

"What if I offered to work free for two weeks," Colton said, "in exchange for a holster an' belt I'll make myself?"

"You know how to make a saddle?"

"No, but I made pretty much everything else we needed on the farm, bridles, harnesses, knife sheaths, anything small. I can take the small stuff out of your way while you work on the saddles."

"What's your name, son?"

"Colton Bonner, sir."

"Well, Colton, since it won't cost me nothin' to try you out, you got a deal. But you do your own holster work on your own time, after we close. An' if you don't do a good job for me, out you go, holster or no holster. Got it?"

"Yes, sir."

At the end of his two weeks, Colton had completed a holster that fit his Colt like a glove, and sat in front of his left hip at a level and an angle that placed it in the crook of his lap. This put the butt of the gun within easy reach of a relaxed and casually placed right hand (or even a left hand if need be), whether that hand was holding his reins, resting on his saddle horn or hooked in his belt. It should afford a quick and easy draw, taking only one fluid motion to draw, point and fire; especially, he realized, if you were standing with your right side mostly facing your opponent, creating a narrower target. He also had made a cartridge belt with loops all the way around it. Even though his colt was a cap-and-ball revolver, he had seen some like it which had been converted to accept metal cartridges. This would mean faster reloading and more efficient ammunition storage, and he wanted to have his Colt converted as soon as he could manage it.

Something else had occurred to him during the two weeks. If he was going to have his Colt converted, it would take a while and he would need a pistol to carry until it was finished. He wanted one of a larger caliber, which meant he would need an additional holster, maybe even sized for a pistol slightly larger than his Colt. One of the conventional hip holsters Mr. Allen had already made would do. With this, he would eventually be able to carry two guns, one on his right hip and one across his belly inside his coat. This could give him two advantages: extra firepower and, if he kept his second gun under his coat, possibly an element of surprise.

"Well, Mr. Allen, my two weeks are up and I have my outfit. If you're satisfied, it's time for me to be be movin' on. One more thing, though. I'd like to buy one of the holsters you already have made."

"Son, you've done a good job for me. You've 'bout caught up my work, so I'll tell you what; you can have that plain holster there in the window. Havin' trouble sellin' it anyway. It's not fancy enough for these wild cowboys with trail money in their pockets."

"Thanks, Mr. Allen! Thanks for everything."

"You ever get back this way an' want a job, a payin' job, you come look me up."

CHAPTER 3

As Colton was leaving Ellsworth, he stopped at an emporium and found a Henry rifle. He bought it and two boxes of ammunition to go with it, and felt much better equipped for the trail. He followed the Smoky Hill River west out of town and headed for the Western Trail, where he might find a herd bound for Nebraska. He was told that they drove cattle into and through Ogalalla to start and supply new ranches further north and west. He could earn some money to buy a new pistol and have his old one converted to use cartridges, and maybe even find a ranch to hire onto when he got there.

He found a herd headed north and, when he told the trail boss about his short time with Hank Benson's herd, and what Hank had said to tell the next trail boss, Arn Jeffords said, "I know Hank Benson. If he was satisfied with ya, I reckon you'll do. We'll prob'ly need ever' man we kin git. We're goin' through Injun country, Pawnee, Cheyenne. We might not see no trouble, but we might."

Colton had just turned sixteen, considered a man by most western standards. He had matured well, sure enough, not only in physical strength and stamina, but in wisdom as well. Hard work and responsibility will do that to a boy. This trip up the trail to Ogalalla would wear away whatever may have remained of the boy in young Colton.

The first incident came while passing through Cheyenne territory. They hit while the herd was strung out over a mile of trail. The men riding point saw them coming and whistled to the men behind them, who passed the whistle all the way back to the drag riders. By the time the Cheyenne attacked, the cowboys had been able to form up well enough to mount a good defense. It was a small scouting or hunting party, but there were enough of them to be dangerous.

As it was, only one cowboy, the one they called "Utah," got an arrow through his thigh, but they emptied seven Indian ponies. The other two managed to get away with a half dozen head of cattle, which had scattered in all the gunfire, and the cowboys considered themselves lucky. As they patched up Utah's leg wound, he turned to Colton and said, "Thanks, kid. He would've got another one in me if you hadn't shot him first."

13

Another, Wes Alder, said, "Yeah, an' I saw ya git two more. That was some good shootin', kid. Where'd you learn ta handle a rifle like that?"

He simply said, "If I didn't hunt, I didn't eat."

From then on, if any of the men had any doubts about Colton being a man, those doubts disappeared. The men all saw Colton in a new light and treated him with the respect due an adult. As for Colton, he saw himself in a bit of a new light as well, and he had mixed emotions about it. On the one hand, it had given him the confidence to face future trouble. On the other hand, he now knew he was capable of taking a human life.

Some would say that it was only an Indian, but Colton didn't see it that way. He had killed a man, and he had to come to terms with that. Not that he regretted doing it; he understood only too well the obvious necessity of defending himself and his companions. No, he didn't regret doing it, he only regretted *having* to do it. That feeling would become all too familiar to him over the years.

After regathering the herd scattered by the Cheyenne, they started back up the trail. Things went relatively well for a while, until they crossed over into Nebraska. They were challenged on the trail by six men who looked to be pretty hard cases. Arn Jeffords rode up to meet them. "There a problem?"

"Yeah. This is our range yer gittin' ready ta cross. Them cattle gonna eat up a lot of the grass our cattle need. We figger yer gonna owe us a few head in return."

"That so?"

"Yeah, that's so."

"Well, I know this is open range, so you boys just move aside." By this time, a couple of the cowboys had seen the riders and guessed what was going on. They had moved up and spread apart a bit, each watching a different rider. Colton quickly picked up on what was developing, but kept his eyes on the man speaking, who seemed to be in charge of the herd cutters. He knew that, if trouble started, it would start with that one.

That man looked around and saw only four cowboys (and one of them just a kid with no gun showing) to his six riders, and said, "Yer a little shy. Maybe you jist better let us cut a few head an' we'll be on our way."

"Maybe you just better go bother another herd." Arn saw the man's hand drop for his gun and he reached quickly for his own. He was faster than the other man, but hadn't quite cleared leather when he heard a gun go off! He thought his gun had fired in his holster until he saw the herd cutter jerk and fall out of the saddle.

The shot had come so suddenly that the other herd cutters were frozen in mid draw! Arn looked around and saw a thin tendril of smoke rising from Colton's pistol, which was now pointed at another of the herd cutters. The other cowboys had, by this time, drawn their Colts also and were covering the awestruck rustlers. They were brought back to reality by Colton's voice. "Your boss is dead. You can join 'im or take 'im home. Your choice, but choose now."

One of the rustlers said to Colton, "He was fast, but I never even seen you draw." Colton's new crossdraw holster had been hidden under his vest and his hand had been on the saddle horn, close, but not obvious. If any of the herd cutters had been watching him, they would have seen no gun on his hip and probably assumed, as the dead rustler had, that this kid was unarmed. Shaken, one rustler dismounted and lifted the body over the empty saddle.

As they silently rode away, Arn looked at Colton and said, "Boy, you just saved our bacon. An' that was the fastest I ever seen a gun drawn. How'd you do that?"

"Just practice," he said, but he also knew the holster had a lot to do with it. And now he had killed his second man.

CHAPTER 4

They had no more trouble on their way to Ogalalla and Colton was glad to have that drive behind him. He was also glad to get paid and, while the others headed for the saloons, Colton went in search of a gunsmith. He found one and started looking over his inventory.

"Lookin' for somethin' in particular?" the proprietor asked.

"Yes, sir, a couple of things. First, I'm interested in a cartridge revolver, but I want a larger caliber than the .36 I've got."

"I've got somethin' new over here. It's Colt's 'New Model Holster Pistol' in .44 caliber. Just came out. Factory-made to take metallic cartridges." He took it out of the display case and handed it to Colton, who looked it over well and tested its action.

"Feels good. Can I try it out?"

"Yeah, we can go right out the back. I got a target set up out there."

After firing a few rounds, Colton said, "This'll do just fine. I'll need ammunition, too. I've got an old cap-and-ball rifle I'd like to trade. I also want to convert my Colt

Navy to take cartridges an' I'll be needin' ammunition for it, too. Can you convert the revolver?"

"Sure, I've done it a few times. It'll take a few days, though. You gonna be in town long?"

"As long as it takes, I reckon. Can we make a deal?"

"Sure. Let's get everything but the conversion settled now and we can worry about the conversion when it's done."

They came to an agreement and Colton left wearing his new .44 Colt in the hip holster he had gotten in Ellsworth. Knowing his biggest purchases were mostly behind him now, he felt he could spare the money for a drink, a good meal and a hotel room.

As he entered the first saloon he came to, he saw a couple of the riders from the drive, and they gave him a very vocal welcome. They began to recount to anyone who would listen the two incidents Colton was involved in on the trail. It made him very self-conscious, for two reasons. To begin with, he wasn't used to the shower of compliments and was self-conscious, especially because of how he had earned them in this case. More importantly, though, he was concerned about getting a reputation that some might want to challenge.

He finished his drink as quickly as he could without seeming rude and went to find a place to eat a quiet meal. He first looked in the window of the restaurant to see if any more of his companions were there. Not seeing any, he went in, sat down and ordered. While waiting for the food, he reflected on the direction his life was taking.

He liked being active in the outdoors, but he was quickly finding out that riding the cattle trails had a number of disadvantages, not the least of which was getting only four hours or so of sleep at night. Hazards such as prairie dog holes, thunderstorms and stampedes were unavoidable, but gun battles were something he could control, or at least try to. If he kept to the cattle trails, he could expect to encounter more of that kind of trouble, so he thought about looking for a ranch to hire onto. He thought that might give him a life he liked, without the confrontations he didn't like.

He was beginning to see evidence of something else he would like to avoid. The days were getting shorter now and the nights were getting chilly. Soon, winter would arrive and the further north he was, the worse the winters would be. He decided he would do well to head south as soon as his pistol was ready and search for a ranch in warmer country.

After a good night's sleep in a soft bed up off the ground, and a good breakfast cooked on a stove rather than a campfire, he decided to go by the gunsmith's shop and see if the man could tell him how long he might have to wait for his conversion to be finished. As was usually the case with him, once he had made a decision, Colton was always anxious to get on with it.

In answer to his question, the gunsmith said, "Well, I got some folks ahead of ya, but if I worked on yours first, it'd prob'ly take three or four days. But if you're in a hurry, a cowboy come in after you left yesterday needin' money an' sold me a Colt Navy that was already converted. I haven't tried it out yet, but it looks to be in good shape, at least as good as yours."

Colton said, "Can we go out back an' try it out?" It shot well, aimed accurately and the workmanship looked very good. He made the trade and walked out ready to start south with the next sunrise.

CHAPTER 5

To keep from going through the Indian Nations, Colton decided to head west first, then turn south once he got into Colorado. As he rode, Colton began to think about his future. He had figured on hiring onto a ranch and continuing to work with cattle, but realized that working on someone else's ranch would only be a short-term plan. If he stayed with cattle, he would want to eventually have his own ranch. Of course, there were other options, but as he went over them in his mind, the indoor jobs just didn't appeal to him. He liked working out in the open air and landscape. The other outdoor jobs he thought about were pretty much dead-end jobs, but at least cattle could lead somewhere. So, he would get further south and start looking for ranches.

Over time, he found several and worked his way south, making both friends and enemies along the way. The friends he strove to make were mostly older, more experienced men; men who had learned more, not only about their jobs, but about

21

life in general, especially about the kinds of people you would encounter throughout life. Colton realized that, the more he knew about people and how they thought and acted, the more advantage he would have. He wanted all the edge he could get when it came to dealing with people, especially people who might oppose him, because the enemies he made were usually rustlers.

His knowledge of people was invaluable when it came to dealing with rustlers. Some of the ranches he worked for had considerable problems with rustlers and Colton tried to put himself in their minds to figure them out. He began to notice personality traits common to most rustlers and soon could almost pick one out of a crowd. He figured out who to watch closely, many times even cowhands on the ranch he was working for, and tried to anticipate their moves. Consequently, he became quite good at catching rustlers before they had a chance to dispose of the stolen cattle, sometimes even before they could get the cattle very far from the herd. As a result, his name got around and before long, he was in demand as a range detective.

This was something he hadn't anticipated, but he found he liked the work very much. The environment suited him well, the hunt was challenging and he was his own boss. And he soon found he could pick his cases, ones that promised to be the most interesting. But the most fulfilling aspect was knowing that he was making a positive difference, catching criminals and protecting the livelihoods of the ranchers and the people who depended on them.

The only thing he didn't like was when the rustlers challenged him. Not that he was afraid; he could usually anticipate their actions and react quickly enough to get the upper hand, and his speed and skill were sufficient to handle the challenges he faced. No, he just didn't like being forced to resort to violence to stop them. A lot of people would still be alive if they hadn't made violence their first choice of resistance. But, when faced with that situation, Colton never hesitated to do what was necessary to protect himself and others from violent people.

As he worked his way down into New Mexico, Colton followed the Rio Pecos for a while, seeing more towns than ranches, but managed to find work in various places as a ranch hand and as a range detective. Again, his name got around as a good man with a gun, and also as a man who could outsmart thieves.

Occasionally, a rustler had the good sense to know when he was caught with no way of getting away from Colton, and preferred to take his chances in court rather than challenge Colton's gun. It was on one of those occasions that Colton was bringing a rustler, along with the body of his partner, into the town of Sena. The prisoner was only seventeen, considered a man by western standards, but still just an impressionable boy.

Colton found the Town Marshal's office, but couldn't find the Marshal. He did, however, find the cell keys in a desk drawer and got the boy into a cell. He then went into the store next door and asked the storekeeper if he knew where Colton could find the Marshal. "We don't have one anymore. The last one got killed tryin' to stop a drunken bar fight an' we don't have anyone else who wants to take on the job."

"Well, I just brought in a rustler an' locked 'im up in the jail. Is there anybody who could take care of 'im 'til the Judge comes around next time?"

"Got no judge, either; least haven't seen one in quite a while. Guess we're so small, they forgot about us. Who is this rustler?"

"Didn't ask his name. If he's local, would you recognize 'im?"

24

"Might. Let's go see this fella." They walked over to the jail and, when the clerk saw the prisoner, he said, "Yeah, I know the boy. You sure he was rustlin'?"

"Caught him an' his partner with a 'Lazy S' steer tied down an' a runnin' iron in the fire. When I challenged 'em, his partner went for his gun. He's tied across his horse out front."

The storekeeper said to the boy, "Tommy, what in the world were you doin'? You know better than this!"

"I know, Mr. Jameson, I guess I just got caught up in it an' wasn't thinkin' straight. Stillwell kept talkin' 'bout how much money he was makin', buildin' his own 'Hat' brand herd from 'Lazy S' cattle an' sellin' 'em over in Santa Fe. An' he said the 'Lazy S' was so big, they wouldn't notice an' he had a fella in Santa Fe that didn't ask no questions, so there wasn't no chance we'd get caught. Guess he found out the hard way that wasn't so."

Colton said, "So, if this Stillwell was sellin' cattle in Santa Fe, he must have a place where he keeps his rustled stock 'til he's got enough to sell, an' prob'ly men there to help 'im. You know anything about that?"

"Yeah, I could take you right to it. He's got two other men there helpin' 'im."

"You know anything about the man in Santa Fe?"

25

"No, he never told me anything about him."

Mr. Jameson turned to Colton and said, "Let's go out into the office an' talk a bit." When seated at the Marshal's desk, Jameson said, "I know this boy. He comes from a good family. He's never been in any kind of trouble before. I know Stillwell, too. He'd lead anybody astray. If Tommy leads you to Stillwell's place so you can get the other men an' get back whatever of the 'Lazy S' cattle that might still be there, you think maybe you could give the boy a break an' let 'im go? I figure this little run-in will cure 'im of wantin' to do this again an', besides, there's nobody to tend to the jail anyway."

"Well," said Colton, "I was hired by the 'Lazy S' to stop the rustlin'. To see that's done, I'll have to clean out Stillwell's place. If this boy helps me do that, it'll help his case. Soon as I drop Stillwell's body off at the undertaker's, I'll go out to the 'Lazy S' an' talk to Ab Sanderson. It won't be up to me, but if this stops the rustlin', he might be okay with that deal."

"Good! You ride on out to the 'Lazy S'. We'll let Tommy stew in that cell for awhile. I'll be in the store when you get back."

CHAPTER 6

When Colton returned from the 'Lazy S', he went first into Jameson's store to tell him of the results of the discussion at the ranch. "They know the boy, too," Colton said. "Sanderson's willin' to overlook the boy's part in it, but only if he helps catch the others an' get the cattle back."

"Good!" said Jameson. "I think the boy will turn out all right."

"My concern," said Colton, "is whether I can trust the boy at Stillwell's place. I don't want to have to worry about him behind me, especially if there's trouble. You reckon there'd be somebody willin' to go out there with me?"

"Can't blame you for playin' it safe. There might be somebody in town that would be willin' to go," Jameson said. "Don't know if they'd risk gittin' into a gun fight with hard cases, but surely, somebody would be willin' to keep an eye on the boy."

"I don't figure to need any help with two rustlers, but I'd feel better with somebody just to keep an eye on the kid. I didn't want to recruit any of the 'Lazy S'

27

hands; they might be a little too quick to make these boys pay for their crimes, if you know what I mean. We don't need them makin' it worse than it already is. Will you see if you can find somebody to go with me, while I talk to the kid?"

"Sure. By the way, who should I say they'll be sidin'?"

"Colton Bonner."

Jameson hesitated just the slightest instant and said, "Yeah, I think I've heard of ya. I'll be back in a little bit."

Colton went back to the cells to talk to Tommy. "Son, I've had a long talk about you with Jameson an' with Ab Sanderson out at the 'Lazy S' an' here's the deal. I want you to lead me to Stillwell's place an' help me drive the cattle back to the 'Lazy S'. I don't expect you to help me get the men who helped Stillwell, but I want you to identify 'em an' testify against 'em in court. If you do that, an' promise never to get into any more trouble, I'll give you a break an' turn you loose."

Tommy's eyes flew wide open and he quickly said, "Yes, sir! I'll take you right to it! I'd help you get those men too, but I'm no hand with a gun. But I can sure help you get those cattle back to the 'Lazy S'! Thanks mister. You don't have to worry about me gettin' into any more trouble, either. Sittin' in this cell all day thinkin' about a rope around

28

my neck has surely cured me of that!"

"Well, you'll spend the night in that cell too, but come dawn, things should get a little better for you."

As Colton left the cell block, Mr. Jameson was coming in the front door. "I found somebody willin' to side you to Stillwell's. Name's Jack Walker. We call 'im 'Flapjack' 'cause he's such a good cook. He owns Flapjack's Restaurant down the street."

"I know of 'im," said Colton, "I've heard 'im mentioned on the cattle trails. Everybody says he's the best chuckwagon cook ever come up the trail. B'lieve I'll drop down there for supper. Tommy," he called back toward the cells, "I'll bring you some supper when I come back."

The first thing Colton noticed as he entered Flapjack's was the aroma of fresh coffee, fresh yeast bread and apples. It seemed Jack's reputation might be well deserved. It was a bit past normal suppertime and most people had already eaten and left, but a few lingered over coffee and dessert, apple pie no doubt. A waitress who looked as if she had been around good restaurants for quite a while greeted him at the door. "Would you like a table in a corner?"

"Is it that obvious?" he asked.

29

"If you know what to look for," she replied, with a smile that put him at ease, "and I've seen enough to know. You'll want coffee as well." She set a menu down and went to the kitchen.

"Well," he thought to himself as he looked over the menu, "ol' Flapjack has expanded his repertoire well beyond chuckwagon fare." However, he was glad to see all the old standards a cowboy wants to sit down to. When the waitress came back with his coffee, Colton ordered a steak, seasoned fried potatoes and fried apples, with some of that fresh bread he had smelled and plenty of butter. "And ask Jack if he has a minute to talk with me. My name's Bonner."

"I figured," she said. "I heard Jack an' Ed Jameson earlier an' it wasn't hard to spot you when you came in. I don't mean any offense; it's just that, as I said, I know what to look for. I'm sure Jack'll be out here just as soon as he can leave the stove."

"Thanks."

He had finished the steak and potatoes and was piling the last of the apples onto the last yeast roll, when Jack Walker came out of the kitchen with a coffee pot and a plate full of sliced peaches. Don't git much fresh fruit on the trail," he said, "figgered you'd like these."

"You figured right! Your food has lived up to your reputation. I bet the trail hands are sure missin' you!"

"Well, I ain't missin' the trail at all. Oh, it wan't a bad life fer a young, restless cowhand, but nobody's young ferever. Got so's a chuckwagon seat was easier on my backside than a buckin' cayuse an' cookin' was easier on my back than ropin' a rank longhorn what didn't wanna be roped. Then it got to whur sleepin' on the ground didn't agree with my ol' bones, so I figgered it was time to do my cookin' in one spot, under a roof with a soft bed."

"Did Mr. Jameson explain everything to you?" Colton asked.

"Yep. I heered you was in the territory. I know a bit about you, too, son. You know how word gits aroun' on the cattle trails. I know 'bout how yer chain lightnin' with a pistol, a crack rifle shot an' how you don't give no quarter to a rustler or herd cutter when they figgered ta run a blazer on ya. But I also heered you'd give a fella a break, if he deserved one. Like that Mason kid ya got up there in that jail."

"He's just a kid who made a mistake," Colton said, "that's all. But, just the same, I don't want 'im behind my back when trouble comes. I just need someone to keep an eye on 'im while I deal with the rustlers. You

31

won't have to get into the fight, if there is one."

"I'll be glad ta do that, but if there *is* trouble, I'll have ta be honest with ya, I might not be able ta stay out of it. Ain't been in a good fight in quite a spell an' the temptation jist might be too much."

They both grinned and Colton said, "It's my fight, my responsibility, but if I need help, I got a feelin' there'd be nobody better to depend on. I'd heard about your cookin' but I've also heard about some of the troubles the outfits you rode with ran into. Your name was mentioned quite a bit and I never heard anything bad. I'll be glad to have you along. We'll leave at first light."

CHAPTER 7

As they rode northwest out of Sena, Colton questioned Tommy about the setup at Stillwell's place. "It's just a little cabin, prob'ly an old line shack, an' two corrals, one for horses and a bigger one for the cattle. They always keep two horses apiece, so if the two men are there, there'll be five horses in the corral. The shack has one door an' one window, both on the front wall, facin' the trail in. I never saw another way into the place."

Colton said, "Well, there'll be another way in, prob'ly from the back, 'cause they'll want another way out. You stop us before we get within sight of the place an' we'll circle around 'til we find it. Then you two stay there with the horses an' I'll slip in on foot. If one gets by me, Jack, you can have 'im.

"If one or both of 'em is there an' they got a fire goin', I'll climb up on the roof an' stop up the chimney. I'm hopin' they won't come out 'til I've had time to jump down an' cover the front door. If they're *not* there, we'll try to track 'em. They might be out rustlin' an' we can catch 'em red-handed, then we can come back later for the cattle."

When they came to a bend in the trail, Tommy stopped them and said, "The shack's about fifty yards ahead." They started circling around through the woods, looking for the back way in. When they found it, they dismounted and Colton opened his saddlebag and brought out a pair of moccasins.

As he sat on a fallen tree trunk and put them on, he said, "You two stay here an' watch for anyone tryin' to get away. I'm gonna look around a bit before I do anything, so it might be fifteen or twenty minutes before anything happens." He slipped silently into the trees and disappeared.

As the shack came into view, Colton found what he was hoping for. There were five horses in the corral, smoke was coming from a small flue and the smell of bacon hung in the air. It didn't surprise him that rustlers would be having breakfast this far into the morning; they worked at night more often than in the daylight.

Keeping to the trees, he made his way around to bring the front of the shack into view. He noticed that the door opened inward, with the latch on his left. This meant that when someone inside opened the door to peek out, they would not be able to see much to their right. After stopping up the flue, he would circle around to the front to put himself at their right, possibly giving himself more of an advantage.

He slipped back around to the side where there was a stack of firewood and picked up a piece of tree limb about the size of the flue diameter. Using a rain barrel as a step, he climbed to the roof, his moccasins muffling his footsteps. He jammed the tree limb into the flue, jumped down and ran to the front corner of the shack with his gun drawn.

It didn't take long for the door to fly open, and the first man, after a brief glance around, emerged. Colton yelled, "Hold it!" but the man made the mistake of going for his gun. It was his final mistake. Colton then called to the other man, "You'll have to come out sooner or later. Better come out now, with empty hands up high."

Very slowly, the man came out and said, "Don't shoot, mister." He was a younger man, not much older than Tommy, and obviously not very eager to end up like his partner. Colton called for Jack and Tommy to come to the cabin, while he made sure the boy had no other weapons on him and that there was no one else in the cabin.

As Jack and Tommy saddled two horses, Colton questioned the boy about their operation. "We was 'bout ready to make another drive to Santa Fe an' was wonderin' where Tommy an' Stillwell was. We figgered they'd got caught, so Albert there decided we might oughtta leave right after breakfast an' just keep goin'. If you'd-a been a half-hour later, we'd-a been free an' clear."

"No," said Colton, "you'd've only delayed your capture and prob'ly got hung in the process. You're better off here with me than you would've been out there with the 'Lazy S' cowhands. Stillwell was no smarter than Albert here. Tommy was smart; smart enough to come clean an' lead us here. He'll get a break because of that. How smart are you?"

"If you'll give me a break, I'll do whatever you say. This is the only rustlin' I ever done. I don't wanna hang for it!"

"Tell me about Santa Fe," Colton said. "Who do you sell to? How does he get rid of the stolen cattle? Who else is involved in the ring?" The boy explained what little he knew, which wasn't much. He knew the name of the man they sold to and where his operation was located, but nothing else. He knew nothing about who else may be selling the man stolen cattle or how the man disposed of them. They hadn't been over there for a couple of weeks, so he didn't know what might be happening there now. The boy seemed genuinely frightened and

Colton was sure he was telling the truth. He was also sure that the boy could be persuaded to find another way of earning a living.

"All right," Colton said. "Since you've been honest with me, I might be willin' to let you go. But if I do, I better not ever see you in this territory again! An' if I ever catch you stealin' cattle again, or even hear of it, I'll hang you myself!"

"Yes, sir! You'll never see or hear from me again!"

"Good. Now, as one last reminder of where this life will lead you, put your partner's body over his horse an' tie it down. Then head for 'out' like your tail was on fire an' don't stop 'til the sun goes down."

At the 'Lazy S' ranch, Colton explained to Ab Sanderson about the rustling operation, the dead rustlers and the boy giving him the name of the man in Santa Fe. "I don't know how many of your cattle they stole altogether, but we managed to bring twenty-three head back, along with the rustlers' horses. You might as well have them, too. The Mason boy was a big help to us. I don't think he'll do any more rustlin' from now on. The only thing left is this man in Santa Fe. It doesn't look like we'll be able to catch him with any of your cattle by this time, so there's not much we'll be able to do about him. At least your trouble with these rustlers is over for a while, though."

"Don't you worry about that man in Santa Fe," Ab said, "I'll pay him a visit an' make sure he knows I intend to talk to the Town Marshal an' the Sheriff over there, an' all the ranchers around. That oughtta put a stop to his ring. An' maybe the Marshal will be able to catch him with some burned-over brands from somewhere else. You done a good job, Bonner. You're expensive, but you cost me a lot less than those rustlers did. Thanks."

CHAPTER 8

On their way back from the 'Lazy S', Jack said to Colton, "Y'know, Ed 'n' me had a talk last night about you. While we been gone, he was a-gonna talk to the others around town. We been needin' a Town Marshal fer a while now. If'n it's okay with the others, would you consider takin' the job?"

Colton thought for a minute and said, "I don't know, Jack. I don't know much about the law, except what little I've learned concernin' cattle."

"Ya wouldn't have ta know too much about the law ta begin with, we mainly jist need someone ta keep the peace. We don't have a lotta what you'd call 'crime' other than whut concerns cattle. Mostly it's just cowboys stoppin' by on a trail drive er comin' in town on payday. They kin git purty rowdy an' shoot up the place right bad, even kill a man from time ta time. We jist need someone ta do some tamin' wunst in a while. Since the last Marshal was killed, we're beginnin' ta git a reputation as a wide-open town. We need ta put a stop ta that afore it gits inny worse. If'n we don't git a handle on it soon, first thing ya know, we'll have outlaws movin' in an' takin' over."

"Well, I don't know, Jack. I'd like to think on it awhile before I could answer that."

"Well, we'll have ta talk ta Ed inyhow an' see whut the folks in town said afore we could hire ya inyway. You think on it an' we'll talk later."

"Okay. I don't have another job lined up just yet, so I'm in no hurry to move on. We'll talk about it tomorrow, after I've slept on it."

"Fair enough."

The next morning, as Colton sat over breakfast in Flapjack's Restaurant, Jack came out of the kitchen long enough to ask him if some of the townspeople could meet with him at the Marshal's office later in the day. They agreed on a time and Colton began to review his thoughts from the night before.

He had never had much reason to consider a career as a lawman. Even though he had spent a few years as a range detective, he never thought about that in terms of the law. It was just a job, helping ranchers keep what was theirs; what they had invested a lot of money, time and work in; helping to preserve the livelihoods of not only the ranchers, but also the cowhands who depended on them for their living. But, what was the job of a lawman anyway? It, too, was protecting the livelihoods of the townspeople, with the added responsibility of occasionally protecting their lives. The rustlers he had tracked down and captured, or sometimes killed, were thieves, trying to take cattle they were not entitled to away from their honest, hard-working owners. Outlaws of any other kind were also just thieves. They stole property or money, which quite often meant stealing opportunities for people's future. Even murderers were just thieves; they stole lives.

Even if a person lost no money, property or life to a thief, they would still lose; they would lose the freedom and liberty to live out the potential that this still-young nation had to offer. It may sound odd, but there can be no freedom, no liberty without restraint. Without the restraint of the rule of law, there is no freedom, only fear. Without the rule of law, we would all be held captive by the brutality of those who would have their way at the expense of everyone and everything else. The strong would enslave the weak. No, if a free society is to endure, there must be the restraint provided by the rule of law.

And if a man refuses to live within that rule of law, refuses to allow that society to live free from fear and oppression, he must be removed from that society. The preferred option is removal to prison, but if the offender violently resists that option, a more drastic removal may be required. The loss of a life, even an outlaw's life, is a tragedy, but without that removal, the future may be even more tragic. Colton understood this. He always preferred the peaceful option, but would not hesitate if the violent option were forced upon him.

Ed Jameson took charge of the meeting that afternoon and began by explaining the current situation in Sena, which was just as Jack had described to Colton the day before. "So, you can see why we're so concerned and anxious to find a Marshal as soon as possible. The main problem is, we're a small town and don't have a lot of money. No one wants to take the job for what we can pay, but we think we've come up with a solution to that.

"The County Sheriff is way over in Las Vegas an' he don't have any deputies over this way. If he hired you, you'd have wider jurisdiction an' the authority to track down our problems an' make arrests outside of town. The Sheriff hires deputies on a pay-per-arrest basis, so it really wouldn't cost him anything extra to hire you. You'd have a base pay from the town an' extra pay from the county on top. We've wired him about it an' should hear back soon."

"Did you mention my name?" Colton asked.

"Yes. We thought maybe he'd heard of you an' if he's heard the same things Jack here has, we thought it might help."

"I've brought 'im a couple of customers from time to time an' he seems to be a good man. If I took this job, I could work for 'im okay. Let me think on it while you're waitin' for his reply. In the meantime, there's some things you'll need to think about, too.

"If I take this job, there'll have to be some conditions. First, I'll need to know who I'm workin' for, Mayor, Council, Citizens Committee, whoever. An' I'll need to know I have the backin' of every business an' business owner in town, bar none. I won't ask 'em to like me, just support me. Next, I'll need the authority to make some rules of my own, based on my own judgment an' experience. Then, I'll need to pick someone to train to be my replacement. That'll take time, but sooner or later, you'll get tired of me or I'll get tired of you; an' when that time comes, I'll leave, but I want to leave you prepared to carry on with what I've started."

"Sounds reasonable," Ed said. "We'll wait to hear from the Sheriff an' hold another town meetin' to discuss your terms. We'll let you know when we've done that."

In his hotel room, Colton thought about the possibility of being a Town Marshal and Deputy Sheriff. The work really wouldn't be that much different, but the living conditions would. He would be living under a roof, for the most part at least. That meant cooler in the summer, warmer in the winter and sleeping up off the ground on a soft mattress. There would still be plenty of opportunity to ride the open spaces he enjoyed so much, but he would have some kind of a home to return to. He hadn't had that in several years now. Maybe this was just what he needed at this point in his life.

CHAPTER 9

When the approval of the Sheriff came through, Colton became a Deputy Sheriff of San Miguel County and Marshal of the Town of Sena. Thus he began a new career as a lawman. He approached it with the same dedication he had shown for each of his other jobs. He began by letting his common sense guide him until he could study the town, county and territorial laws. He wasn't in a big hurry to learn U.S. laws yet; the U.S. Marshal could worry about that for the time being.

He also studied posters and handbills issued by other law officers regarding criminals in other parts of the territory, memorizing their descriptions and keeping an eye out for them. Those who had committed crimes within his jurisdiction he arrested and held for trial. Those otherwise beyond his authority found their names prominently displayed at each end of town on an order banning them from entry, subject to arrest for trespassing, and ultimately subject to extradition. To these criminals, he gave no quarter.

45

He was a little more lenient with the residents of Sena, however. He knew them to be good citizens, even if some of them did get into their whiskey a bit too much and cause a ruckus now and then. These he let sleep it off in a cell overnight and released them back to their jobs the next morning, with maybe a small fine for disturbing the peace. The townspeople came to regard Colton as a stern but fair peace officer and he soon gained their respect.

This was certainly not the case with most outlaws. Some, of course, did come to admit Colton's fairness and did respect him for it. Most, however, resented his boldness and, when the opportunity presented itself, sought to challenge him. The lucky ones found themselves in jail and eventually in prison. The others, by their passing, built a reputation for this Marshal, a reputation he neither sought nor welcomed. A reputation was a two-edged sword. He knew it would discourage some from making trouble in his town, but he also knew the kind of people such a reputation might attract, and he knew these people would only bring trouble to the town and to himself.

The only alternative, however, was to let those people have their way and this, he knew, was not an option. The West was growing up and eventually would settle down, but that time was still in the future.

Until then, tough lawmen and stern enforcement would be necessary to tame this young land and make it safe for families to settle here and help the country mature. And these lawmen would continue to make enemies among outlaws.

After a couple of years, the town of Sena was quiet and settled, respectful of the law and a good place to raise a family. Only occasionally was its serenity broken. The problem was *why* it was broken. The saloon brawls abated, but the challenges to a Marshal with a reputation for two fast guns began to increase. Colton was not surprised by this. He always recognized its probability, but had hoped against hope that it might pass him by.

He also understood the effect it would have on the townspeople. They began, rightly of course, to look at him as the ultimate cause of these occasional outbursts of violence. Their patience began to wear thin, as he knew it would, and he soon realized it was time for him to move on, for his own sake as well as the town's. He had no illusions of being able to escape a reputation, but he hoped to be able to stay ahead of it, at least for awhile.

His resignation was accepted with a mixture of sadness and relief. Though appreciative of the job he had done, everyone realized the necessity of his leaving, and they knew the town would be in good hands with the man he had chosen as his replacement.

Over the next few years, Colton moved around quite a bit from town to town, from state to state and territory to territory, occasionally taking a job as a lawman or going back to range work. Sooner or later, though, no matter where he went, his reputation would track him down and, after defending himself, he would move on.

As time went by, he found himself thinking more and more about his future. He had grown to like having a home, staying in one place. If a man was to build a future, he could only do it by first establishing a home. He knew he wouldn't be able to settle in one place with his reputation; at least, not in a town, where he might be found by the wrong people, and certainly not as a well-known peace officer. A more likely, and preferable, scenario would be to start a ranch somewhere in the middle of nowhere, where he was not likely to be found.

The more he traveled and the more he thought about it, and the more he had to defend himself against those who sought to challenge his reputation, the more he longed to be able to just drop out of sight and be free of the life his own skills had built for him, free of the legend he had become. The final straw came one day, in one of the many little out-of-the-way towns whose name he would never even remember, with two men whose names he never even knew.

CHAPTER 10

In one of the many small towns he had ridden into, Colton was recruited as Marshal. He had no illusions as to the temporary nature of this job, nor as to the general circumstances under which it would be terminated. What he did not anticipate, however, was the specific reason behind those circumstances. He knew he had a wide reputation within the community of outlaws and gunmen over several states, and he knew many people would be quite relieved if he were out of their way, but he never realized just how badly they wanted that to happen.

In every new town, Colton made it a point very early to familiarize himself with all the faces of the townspeople and any surrounding ranch personnel. He also made a habit of watching the roads into town for any unknown faces coming in. One day, he saw two such faces. He did not recognize the faces, but their type was hard to mistake...rough, dirty, unshaven, trail-worn, with eyes constantly moving. These were not honest cowhands or men looking for honest work.

They had not seen him yet, but he kept track of where they went and checked up behind them, asking if they were known and what, if anything, they had said or asked. Not surprisingly, they had asked some general questions about what kind of town this was and what kind of law enforcement they had. They were looking for him, alright. He would let them find him, but he wanted it to be at a time and place of his own choosing.

His preference would be to meet them out in the open, away from bystanders; hopefully both men together, but one at a time if he could be sure of the whereabouts of the other. They made that decision for him, splitting up and making it harder for Colton to keep track of them both. He soon realized he would have to focus on only one at a time, hoping the other would not pop up behind his back unexpectedly. They also made the decision for him as to when and where it would happen.

The showdown came one morning as Colton was about to come out of his office. He heard a man yelling from up the street for him to come out. He thought of going out the back door and slipping up on them, but he realized the two men would probably have planned for that. The second man

51

would no doubt be waiting out back to catch him off guard. Colton would have to do some fast thinking to keep 'Backdoor Man' from sneaking up on him while he dealt with the other.

He opened the front door and stood on the threshold, just far enough out to answer the man, but not far enough to be a target. He looked across the street at the windows in the front of the dry goods store. In them, he could see the reflection of the gaps on either side of the Marshal's Office, separating it from the buildings on each side. The gaps were empty so far.

"What do you want?" Colton yelled. If he could convince 'Backdoor Man' that he intended to come out the front door, 'Backdoor Man' should come out of his hiding place behind the office to position himself either behind Colton from the one side, or beside him from the other side, as he walked up the street toward his challenger.

"I want you," the man responded. "You're gonna make me rich!"

Colton didn't like the sound of that. He knew of only one way he could make the man rich. "How's that?" he asked.

"There's a $5,000.00 bounty on your head."

"I haven't broken any laws," Colton said, taking another step out the door, hopefully making enough noise for 'Backdoor Man' to hear what he was doing.

"No, but you've made a lot of enemies an' they decided to deal with you the same way you've dealt with them."

"I should've been expecting this," Colton thought to himself. This was not unheard of, but he never thought of himself as qualifying for it. Another loud step out the door brought the results Colton desired. 'Backdoor Man' must have thought Colton's attention was focused completely on the man up the street, and he took it as an opportunity to slip up beside the Marshal's Office to put himself behind Colton. Colton saw this reflected in the window across the street. Leaving the front door standing open, he slipped out the back door and quickly stepped into the gap between the buildings behind 'Backdoor Man'.

'Backdoor Man' peeked around the front corner of the office, but saw nothing. By the time he suspected a trick, Colton was already behind him. The man whirled around to take a shot at anyone he saw behind him, but Colton was ready and made short work of the man.

Hearing the shot and believing the trick worked, the man up the street yelled to 'Backdoor Man'. Instead of hearing a response from his partner, he saw Colton step into the street.

"You've only got two options," said Colton, "surrender or try to draw. Which will it be?"

The man hesitated, but only a moment. "I took the job," he said. "I got no choice."

"Yeah," Colton said, "I know."

They both drew at once and people would later say there was only one shot, but the hole in Colton's coattail said there was a second one. The first one found its mark in the man up the street. He would never get the chance to collect his bounty.

Colton knew from this incident that his time as a lawman and range detective had come to an end. If he stayed, the town would no longer be secure from Marshal-hunting outlaws and, stay or leave, he wouldn't be able to feel secure as a private citizen either. He was no longer willing to allow himself to be a target for any gunhand looking to earn a bounty, but there was no horse fast enough to outrun his reputation. So, he could either spend the rest of his life looking over his shoulder and trying to shoot his way out of deadly situations, or he could just disappear.

He walked back into the Marshal's Office, dropped his badge on the desk and shut the door behind him on the way out. He walked to the Livery Stable, saddled his horse and told the hostler that, for the town's sake as well as his own, he was leaving. "If anyone asks," he said, "I no longer exist."

That was the last anyone saw or heard of the man called Colton Bonner. Some said he met his match somewhere along the trail, but few believed that. Some said he rode down to live out his days in Old Mexico, where nobody knew his name. Some said he just changed his name and started a ranch someplace so remote that he wouldn't be found. Whatever did happen, the name Colton Bonner eventually faded from popular conversation, and his legend faded with it.

EPILOGUE

"You seem to know an awful lot about this Colton Bonner," I said to the old man. "Was he still living when you were a kid? Did you ever know him?"

"Know 'im?" He got quiet for a moment, his eyes reaching out toward the horizon as if looking for something, maybe looking *at* something, or at some*one*. "Yes...yes, I knew 'im."

"Well, I never heard of the man, but this is real interesting," I said. "I'm a writer and I think Colton's story would make a good book. Could I come back sometime and hear more about him?"

"Sure," the old man said, coming back from the horizon, "there's always more to tell. You come back any time. You can find me right here in this cafe most days."

"Great. By the way, I never did ask your name."

"Hays," the old man said (and I could have sworn I saw just a hint of glimmer in his eye), "Cody Bonner Hays."

56

BOOK 2

A SAGEBRUSH TRAIL

PROLOGUE

It was hot. That brassy sun had scorched this wasteland for centuries, and now it was beginning to work on him. His Appaloosa didn't seem to pay any heed though. That's why he liked this horse so well. It would stick to a trail no matter the weather, terrain or the miles. The man wished he could make the same claim.

If he'd had his choice, he wouldn't be on this trail, but Johnny Longley had made the choice for him. Johnny always did have an oversized sense of his own gun handling skills, and his sense of self-importance was even bigger. So when Johnny saw this stranger wearing two guns, he saw a chance to build his reputation up to a size more comparable to his ego.

Johnny didn't know who this stranger was and didn't care. If he had known, he might have left him alone. But, then again, he might not have. The answer to that doesn't matter anymore, for Johnny ended up face down on the floor of that saloon, his reputation dying with him. And the stranger ended up on this trail to wherever they

58

wouldn't know him, because Johnny had four older brothers. Not that the stranger was worried about the odds; he had faced tough odds before. No, he left because Johnny's father, he was told, was a kindly old man who had loved his youngest son dearly, as he did the other four as well, and this stranger had no desire to bereave the old man any further by taking away the rest of his boys.

So he rode, under a burning sun, on a sagebrush trail to who-knows-where.

CHAPTER 1

He was headed south. He decided that Old Mexico would be a good place for him to wait, to give the Longley brothers time to decide that he wasn't worth wearing out four good horses in a vendetta ride that didn't need to be taken. When they got the story from that bartender back in Mill Creek, they surely would see that he had no choice but to do what he had done, and they would decide to cut their losses and go back home. Any reasonable man would do that. If the Longley boys were ever reasonable though, the loss of their brother had clouded that reason.

A couple of days' ride below the border brought him to the little town of Poca, as small as its name implied. As he rode into town, he decided it looked quiet enough to rest in for a while. His first stop was the stable. He always took good care of his Palouse; it had taken good care of him many times in the past. His next stop would be that cantina across the street, to take care of his empty stomach.

The music inside sounded pleasant, the food smelled good and the tequila was flowing. Yes, he decided he could stay here, at least for tonight. He made his way to an empty table in the corner, where he could sit with his back to the wall. A waitress came by. "*¿Que quieres comidas, Señor?*"

"*Sí, por favor, carne, frijoles y cervesa.*" He sat studying the patrons, particularly looking for anyone who seemed curious about him. He saw nothing to be concerned about, so when the food arrived, he wasted no time in making the best of it and soon was relaxed and enjoying the mariachis.

As they began another song, a murmur throughout the crowd caught his attention and he looked up to see a beautiful, black-haired *señorita* standing by the musicians. All eyes had turned to her, the men's eyes filled with desire, the women's eyes filled with envy. She began to dance. Several of the men tried to get her attention. "Elena! Over here!" "Elena! This way!" She danced around the room, teasing the men as she went. When she came close to this gringo's table, their eyes met...only for a second, but it was long enough. She danced away, but looked back several times as she went.

He always was a sucker for dark eyes. Hers seemed like an abyss a man could fall into forever and never reach bottom. And the way she moved would entice even the most indifferent of men. And she seemed to be trying to catch his eye.

Elena didn't know who this stranger was, but she knew she wanted him. She had had other men before, but this one was different. Why, she couldn't say, but she could feel it. She couldn't take her eyes off him as she danced. Was it her imagination, or did he seem interested also? She had to know.

As she whirled around the cantina floor, she kept working her way back around to him, feeling her attraction build as she approached. The closer she got, the more he seemed to be looking at her. Or was it just her wishful thinking? No, now his eyes met hers, a smile in them, even if not on his lips. She knew he was hers, at least for tonight.

CHAPTER 2

Later, in Elena's room, she studied the stranger's face in the dim light of the small adobe fireplace. "Your eyes, I have watched them, tonight in the cantina. Always, they move, as if you watch for someone... someone you do not want to see. You have enemies, *mi corazón*."

"Yes. I have enemies."

His mind went back to that saloon in Mill Creek, back to that evening he wished he could change. It was like he was perched above the crowd, watching the whole scene play out:

Johnny Longley was intently watching the stranger as he came into the saloon and walked to the bar. He could tell by the way the man constantly eyed the crowd and by the fact that he wore two guns, one on his hip and another across his belly, that here was a man who, if he didn't have a reputation, at least deserved one. Johnny didn't know who the man was, but someone probably would, and they could later tell how Johnny had beat him to the draw. At least, that's how Johnny's ego saw it.

Johnny walked to the bar next to the man and stared at him while the man sipped his whiskey. He stared, but the man didn't acknowledge his attention, which irritated Johnny. And an irritated Johnny Longley always felt an uncontrollable urge to act, usually in a rash manner. He said, "What's your name, mister?"

The stranger slowly turned his eyes to Johnny and studied him for a moment. His name? He had left that behind a few years ago, just as he had left his old life behind. At least he had tried to, but his old life seemed to follow him wherever he went, even if his name did not. His name? "You wouldn't recognize it."

Johnny's irritation grew. He set his whiskey down and took a half step away from the bar. "I asked you a question, mister. You didn't answer it"

The stranger's eyes returned to his drink. "Mostly, folks just call me C.B."

Johnny wasn't accustomed to being taken so lightly. "Well, C.B., we don't like drifters like you in this town, so why don't you just fork your bronc an' ride out!"

"That's just what I had in mind...right after I've had my drink an' some supper."

The irritation now took control of Johnny and he stepped away from the bar

64

and away from C.B. Silence moved through the crowd like a wave, and people quickly began to move back from the two men. C.B. still sipped his drink in silence, which drove Johnny to the edge. C.B. could feel it welling up in Johnny and he tried to convince the boy of the senselessness of it all. "Son, it ain't worth it. You'll be shed of me soon enough. Just let me eat an' I'll be gone."

But it was too late. The stranger's indifference was intolerable to Johnny. "I said get out now!" His hand crept lower, toward the butt of his Colt.

C.B. turned only slightly, glanced down at Johnny's hand and said, "Is a life so cheap that you would end it over a few minutes' difference?"

Fury rose up in Johnny's face! People didn't challenge him, especially not some drifter! His hand snapped the Colt out of its holster and, yes, he was fast...but not fast enough. The muzzle of his gun had not yet come level 'til C.B.'s gun spoke. Johnny's legs sagged and he sank to the floor. C.B. looked at the boy's body, shook his head slightly and whispered, "A waste."

The bartender looked down at Johnny's lifeless form, then turned to C.B. and said, "Mister, I know it weren't your fault, but he was the apple of his papa's eye and that old man would move heaven an' earth for that boy. An' Johnny's got four brothers; an' if you kick one of them Longley boys, the others all holler 'ouch!' If you don't ride out of here pretty quick, you best be prepared to use both them guns."

C.B. looked at the bartender, thought for a moment, sighed and quietly said, "The old man's lost enough today." He turned and slowly walked out.

"Yes," C.B. said, "I have enemies. There are probably four of them looking for me now." He looked down at Elena. "Does that frighten you?"

After just enough hesitation for him to know she had considered it, she replied, "No. If there are four, your enemies are weak. If they were strong, it would not take four. No, you are the stronger one. They are not wolves; they are coyotes. You are the wolf. I do not fear for you, and I do not fear for myself either, being with you. I know you would not harm me. That, also, I see in your eyes."

He smiled and pulled her closer to him. She knew that, come sunrise, he would be saddled and gone, trying to stay a step ahead of his enemies, trying to avoid trouble. She knew she wouldn't be able to convince him to stay; that was not the kind of man he was. Nor could she count on him being able to come back. She knew they had only tonight, so she determined to make the most of it.

The next morning, as C.B. was saddling his horse, Elena asked, "Will I ever see you again?"

His thoughts went to the Longley brothers. "I don't know. There's trouble following me...there always seems to be trouble following me. I keep movin' to try to get away from it, or at least stay ahead of it, but it keeps findin' me somehow. I'm growin' tired of this life, Elena; tired of never bein' able to stop in a town long enough to get to know people, of always lookin' down my back trail, of eatin' meals over a campfire and sleeping on the ground. I've dreamed of settlin' down, startin' a ranch, raisin' sons, but it just never seems to work out that way."

"I could be a good wife to you, *mi corazón*. I would give you sons, strong sons to build your rancho."

He looked at her with hopeful eyes, but he knew deep down it wasn't in the cards. "Who knows? Maybe, when the trouble with the Longley boys is over..."

"Go back and settle this trouble then," she said. "I will be here. Come back if you can."

"I can't guarantee you anything. It may be a long time before trouble stops followin' me. It may never stop. I might not be able to come back at all."

Elena looked at C.B., smiled slightly, and said, "You are stronger than your troubles. You will do what you must, what you can. I will be here."

He mounted and started for the trail, a loneliness already welling up within him, a loneliness he was becoming all too familiar with. He was sure he had just given Elena a false hope, but it was a hope he wanted to feel himself. Maybe he really could get this mess settled and put it all behind him. Maybe...

CHAPTER 3

The Longley boys didn't know who the man was that killed their baby brother, they just knew they were going to even the score. It didn't matter why he did it, it only mattered that it had been done. It might not be easy finding him...they didn't have much to go on, but they had a start.

When they had gotten the news about Johnny, the four brothers immediately mounted their best horses and rode for town. The bartender knew more of the story than anyone else, so they questioned him the most. He was a bit reluctant to tell them much about this stranger who had only defended himself, but he was too afraid of the Longleys not to. So, he told them the whole story, making sure they got the message that Johnny had given the man no choice; but that didn't seem to matter to them. "Jist never you mind who's fault it was, you jist tell us about this stranger. He give a name?"

"Sorta; said most folks just called him C.B."

"What'd he look like?"

69

"Tall, lean, but not skinny, dark hair, moustache, wearin' black with a flat-brimmed hat. He wore two guns, one on his hip and another across his belly."

"You see which way he went, what he was a-ridin'?"

"No, but I heard Clete say he saw 'im take the west road outta town, on a big Appaloosa."

"How long ago?"

"'Bout three hours maybe."

They were well-mounted and their horses could hold a canter all day. Not that they had to be in a hurry, the other ranch hands could handle things 'til they got back, but they were eager to get the job done while the fires in their bellies still burned hot. This man called C.B. had left town on the west road, but that leads to a crossroads, where he could have gone in any of the three other directions.

So they rode hard, stopping at each town they came to, just long enough to ask about a man in black on a big Appaloosa. Sometimes they heard news, sometimes not, but it was enough to steer them to what they thought was the right track. Soon, they kept telling each other...soon.

C.B. couldn't be sure whether the Longley boys were looking for him or not, but he traveled as if they were. He had long ago trained his eyes and ears to travel searching for trouble, either coming up behind him or waiting ahead of him. This trip made that training essential, for his mind was on other things right now. The journey back from Mexico was taking him through Apache country, barren rock and sand, with no waterholes in sight. That didn't mean there wasn't any water, just that the desert was good at hiding it from you. Sometimes, if you were lucky, you might even run upon a rock formation that created a cistern where water would gather, maybe from a seep or even a spring. They were few and far between, but if you knew where to look, you could find one. If you didn't, you could be in real trouble. Why did his journeys always seem to take him through the hottest parts of the country?

Keeping his head on a swivel, he constantly reminded himself that when you couldn't see an Apache, that's when you knew they were around. These denizens of the desert could hide where there was no hiding place to be found, and could cover more ground on foot than a white man could on a horse. And they could fire a dozen arrows about as fast as you can fire twelve rounds from a Winchester. Some even had

Winchesters now, so C.B. kept to open ground as much as possible, in hopes that he could spot any Apaches while they were still beyond the range of their bows, even out of range of the average Winchester; but not of *his* Winchester.

It had cost him almost a month's pay, but his life was worth a lot more, so he had bought one of the new Centennial model Winchesters. Its .45-75 cartridge was capable of putting down a grizzly or a buffalo; maybe not quite at the same distance as the Sharps "Big .50," but its greater rate of fire made up for the difference. To take advantage of its long-distance accuracy, he had put a Vernier sight on it, which was good for farther than his eye could see a target.

Nights in the desert are cold, but he kept his fires small. Apaches didn't like to travel or fight at night, but you could never be sure what an Apache might decide to do. C.B. was a light sleeper anyway, because of the life he lived; but even so, he didn't get much rest, and wouldn't until he was clear of this part of the territory. He was sure looking forward to that.

He was far enough through this part of the country that he was beginning to think he might not see an Apache, when he spotted six off in the distance, toward the northeast, crossing what would be his path. They spotted him about the same time and turned toward him. It was a sure bet the Apaches weren't going to prove friendly. They weren't friendly with many people, including other Indian tribes. Mexicans and Tarahumara Indians were high on their list of enemies, but the white man was at the top. With very few exceptions, they detested the white man for forcing them onto desert reservations, where they had to struggle against harsh conditions and poor soil just to survive; and the meager supplies the white man gave them under the treaty were never enough to fill their needs.

C.B. headed for a rock outcrop just ahead. It had a crevice where he sheltered his horse from possible attack, but he didn't intend to let them come close enough for that. He positioned himself on top of the rock, found a good rest for his Winchester and raised the Vernier sight.

The Apaches were coming faster now, leaving no doubt as to their intentions. Even so, he saw no need to kill if deterrence would work, so he picked a target just ahead and to one side of them, a rock about three or four feet wide, estimated the distance at about 600 yards and set his sight accordingly. He felt sure his Centennial could persuade them of the hopelessness of their efforts.

He touched off a round and watched the dust fly up off the rock. At the "spang" of the ricochet, the Apaches' heads turned quickly toward the rock, and they pulled their ponies to a stop. A few seconds later, when they heard the report from the shot, they turned back toward C.B. He could imagine their conversation as it dawned on them that this white man had shot that close to them from such a distance. They probably had not experienced this kind of accuracy at this distance, and may have been discussing the possibility of luck being involved. To show them that hitting this rock was no accident, he chambered another shell and fired again. The second shot hit the same rock. To drive his point home, he repeated this feat for a third time.

By now, the Apaches realized they would never be able to get within arrow range, or even normal rifle range, of this man over this open ground before his rifle could send them to the Happy Hunting Grounds. They turned and resumed their original path towards the southwest. At least, that's what it looked like; but with an Apache, you never knew. They might have just wanted him to think they were resuming their original journey, hoping he would leave the rocks, and they could circle back and catch him out in the open desert, with *them* in the rocks for cover.

No, thought C.B., he would be safer staying put for a while. He would watch the area to the west and south to see if they showed up again. The sun was getting low in the sky, so he would wait until dark before moving out. By sunup, he should be beyond their reach. Another sleepless night, but maybe soon he would be in safer territory.

Safer, that is, unless you considered the Longley brothers. He had a little time now to consider them. He had run across no sign so far that they were out looking for him, but it could be that they just didn't want to cross Apache country. They may have figured he was headed for Old Mexico in desperation and wouldn't want to risk coming back through there himself; maybe they would call off the search. Or they could have figured he would stay only a while and *would* risk coming back later; they might be waiting in a likely town for him to show up again. Or they could have lost his trail altogether and given up, and he could ride back safely. It was even possible they decided there was no point in chasing a man who was only defending himself in a fair fight...not likely, but possible. No, the only option he had the luxury of considering was that they were waiting somewhere on the trail for him to come back from Old Mexico

Soon he would likely be trading one danger for another.

Well, it was dark now. He might as well get to it.

CHAPTER 4

When he finally came to a town, C.B. stopped at the saloon first. A careful look from the door failed to reveal what he was looking for: four men resembling each other, at a table together, looking like they had ridden a hard trail and watching the crowd expectantly. Even so, he entered carefully and tried to keep an eye out for any undue interest from the patrons. Several people glanced his way, but he didn't see anyone overly interested, so he ordered a drink. As the bartender poured, C.B. asked, "Any strangers in town lately? Besides me, that is," and grinned just enough to hopefully put the bartender at ease.

"No, not many people drift through here. We're kinda off the main trail a bit. Lookin' fer someone in p'ticular?"

"No," C.B. said with another grin, "just wonderin' if anyone's lookin' for *me*."

The bartender returned his grin and said, "Well, not yet anyways."

"How about a hotel or restaurant? Got either in town?" C.B. asked.

"Sure, got both an' a cafe, too. Cafe's a couple doors down on this side of the street, a rest'rant the other end of town. Hotel's 'bout halfway in between. There's a stable 'cross from it."

"Much obliged." C.B. headed towards the stable first. If the Longley boys were in town, they hadn't asked about him. He probably had a little time to eat and listen. If he still didn't hear any talk about strangers, maybe he could try to get some rest in a hotel room.

After stabling his Palouse, he headed for the restaurant down the street. After days of camp food on a rough trail, he was looking forward to a comfortable meal.

The Longley boys rode into that little town of Quinwood just before sundown. The saloon was their first stop, not just because it had been a long, hot, dry trail (it had been), but because that's where you could go in any town to find out anything that was known to anyone. They found a spot at the bar and asked for whiskey and information. "Seen a drifter lately, wearin' black, ridin' a big Palouse? Woulda been wearin' two guns like he knows how to use 'em."

The bartender said, "Don't know 'bout the horse, but seen the man. He came in, had a drink an' asked where was a good place to eat. I mentioned a place or two an' he left." Whatever was between these men and the stranger earlier was none of his business, and he wasn't about to take sides.

"Where was that 'place or two'?"

"Cafe a couple doors down an' a rest'rant the other end of town."

"Thanks." They knocked their drinks back and headed for the cafe first. A good look through the window was enough to show them he wasn't there. He might have been and left, but they would check the restaurant first, in case he might be there. If not, they would ask about him as they retraced their steps back to the saloon.

He wasn't in the restaurant by the time they got there. They stopped a waitress. "Seen a man in black wearin' a two-gun rig, lookin' like he just come off the trail?"

"He was here," she said, "but he's been gone a little while. I have no idea where he would have gone when he left."

They headed back up the street, but there was no sign of him now, even back at the saloon. The oldest brother said, "We ain't likely to find him at night, he could be inywhere. We might as well git a hotel room an' try to git a decent night's sleep. Might be some fresh sign in the mornin'. An', who knows, maybe we'll git lucky an' run into 'im at the hotel." Just in case, they asked the hotel clerk about him. "Yeah, he was here. Started to check in, but left all of a sudden. Guess he heard them two men talkin' about somebody askin' after someone lookin' like him. No clue where he went, though."

The men walked back outside. The oldest said, "He's prob'ly gonna leave, an' we cain't let 'im git away! Let's split up and search the town. We'll look in the stable, but he might figger that's whut we would expect; he could be hidin' somewheres a-hopin' we'll leave town lookin' fer 'im. Look ever'where, 'specially the places you wouldn't expect someone ta be." The brother that decided to look in the livery stable made the mistake of looking there by himself. In a way, he did help their cause, but he paid a high price for it.

Standing quietly in the dark outside the entrance, he could hear some movement inside that sounded like straw on the floor. It could have been a restless horse, but it also could have been a man in a hurry to saddle a horse.

Quietly, he slipped into the stable and stood just to one side of the door...quietly, but maybe not quietly enough. Either that, or he cast just enough shadow going through the doorway to put anyone inside on the alert. Whatever the cause, it was enough to silence the noise he had heard. He was sure it was the man he was seeking, but how to locate him? He remained still, almost afraid to breathe. Waiting was to his advantage; sooner or later, his brothers would make their way here. Waiting was not so good for C.B., however.

C.B.'s voice from the back of the stable finally broke the silence. "You lookin' for me?" At that, Longley thought he had the man located and fired toward the sound. He had him located alright...enough to hit his target, but not precisely enough to finish the job. Longley's powder flare, however, had served to locate himself well enough, and C.B. put an end to the battle with a well-placed shot. But he knew it wouldn't be the end of the war. The gunfire would surely bring the other Longley boys and this one had done enough damage to make finishing the job easy for the rest of them unless he moved quickly.

The burning wound in his side made mounting his horse a painful endeavor, but he knew he had no choice, and little time. He was glad that at least it was dark. His blood trail would be almost impossible to track and soon he would have enough of a lead to stop just long enough to get the bleeding stopped.

When he figured he had a couple of hours and several miles between him and the three remaining Longley brothers, C.B.

stopped, built a small fire and heated water to make coffee and to clean and bandage his wound. He was relieved to find that the bullet had gone through the fleshy part of his side and had missed anything vital. He always carried a small bottle of disinfectant in his saddlebags, but he used it as sparingly as he dared, for there wasn't much left in the bottle. He would have to resupply in the next town he came to. As he worked, he wondered...

How did he always manage to get into these situations? Why did trouble always have to follow him? For a long time, he had dreamed of settling on a small ranch, taking a wife, raising sons. He thought now about Elena, and how she might have made him a good wife, as she had said, might have given him strong sons to help him work a ranch. Maybe, after all this is over, he *could* go back and see Elena. Maybe they could start a little ranch down in Mexico. Or maybe he could bring her back with him and find a little ranch somewhere around here. Maybe, when this is over...but this kind of thing never seemed to be over for him. His dreams would likely remain just dreams.

Then he thought of Old Man Longley and how he had undoubtedly had those same dreams. And now C.B. was the means by which one of those dreams was in the process of being destroyed, one son at a time. The thought of needless violence left him cold these days.

He was tired of the trail, tired of leaving a town because of trouble, tired of having to watch his back trail, even when he knew of no one following him. If he could lose the Longley boys and find a place to settle...the pain of his wound reminded him just how remote that possibility was. After the Longleys, there would no doubt be others. There were always others; and so there would always be other towns.

Disgusted, he rolled into his blanket and tried to sleep.

CHAPTER 5

C.B. had managed to get a little rest in spite of the pain of his wound. He had headed for higher, rocky country which would be better for hiding his tracks. He fully expected the Longley boys to find his blood trail this morning, but hoped they would have a harder time following him once he had stopped the bleeding and hit the rougher ground. He figured he had enough head start on them that he could take a little time to change the dressing on his side. It was still bleeding some, but not enough to leave a trail, and he didn't figure he'd lost enough blood to do more than just slow him down a little.

He brought the embers back to life in his campfire and boiled some water for coffee and began to redress the wound in his side. It looked much better this morning. He had always been a quick healer and the air in this higher altitude would help speed up the process.

He was well aware, though, that he couldn't expect to outrun the Longley boys in his condition, nor could he count on them not being able to track him...he had known trackers good enough to trail a trout upstream. He began to think about his next move. He was heading into more familiar country and knew of no good places anywhere near here to hole up for any length of time. If he had to keep moving, his best bet would be to find a ranch or cabin where he could get supplies, bandages and a poultice for his wound.

As he saddled his Appaloosa, he was thinking about a place he knew a ways off that, if he could make it that far safely, no one following him would be likely to know about. He would head in that direction and see if he could find a place on the way to resupply.

Towards the end of that day, he came upon a ranch which looked like it had seen better days. He pulled the Palouse up to the rail in front of the house and stepped down. As he was tying the horse, a woman came hesitantly out onto the porch. "Can I help you?"

He said, "Could I trouble you for a meal and some bandages, Ma'am?"

She then saw the bloody hole in his shirt and her manner changed at once. "Of course! Come into the house." She helped him up the steps and led him to the kitchen, where she put some water on the stove.

"Take your shirt off and I'll get some bandages." The wound didn't look infected, but she made a poultice for it, just to be safe. "You're healing over pretty good, but I'm sure you could use some rest. I have a spare room you can use, and I'll get you one of my late husband's shirts to wear."

"No," he objected, "I thank you, Ma'am, but there's trouble followin' me an' I need to keep movin'"

"You need to rest!" she insisted. "What kind of trouble?"

"A boy tried to use me to build a reputation. It was self-defense, but that didn't matter to his four brothers. They been followin' me for a while now. They caught up with me in Quinwood an' I had to shoot my way out. I killed another one of 'em, but he got some lead into me in the process."

"So I see," she said. "Well, don't you worry about that. I'll put your horse in the barn and you can hide out here for a while. If they come looking for you, I'll get rid of them. I'll send them off chasing their tails and you'll be safe. I'm Lillian Granville, by the way; what's your name?"

"Just C.B.'ll do. I appreciate your offer, Ma'am, but those men are a hard bunch. They might try to make trouble for you."

"They wouldn't dare make trouble for a widow. I don't care how hard they are, they would know that wouldn't be tolerated. Everyone around knows my husband is dead and they're very protective of me. They would hunt these men down and make them wish they had never seen this territory."

C.B.'s instinct told him he needed to be moving on, but he was still a little weak and tired. After some consideration, he decided he maybe could stay for a little while, at least long enough to get some of his strength back. He may need all the strength he can muster before it's all over with.

Giving him a safe place to lay low was more than he had expected; after all, he was just some drifter who stopped at her ranch looking for a meal and some care for his wound. Dressing his wound would not have been surprising, regardless of who he was. What was surprising was her insistence that he stay, her continued treatment of his wound, cooking for him, giving him one of her late husband's shirts.

As they sat over a meal on his second day there, C.B. asked her about the ranch. "Pardon me for sayin' so, Ma'am, but I've noticed the place could use some work. Don't you have any help?"

"You can just call me Lillian. This used to be a really nice ranch," she said, "but my husband was killed a few years ago and the hands just drifted away over time. I couldn't keep the ranch up alone and had to sell off the cattle little by little to support myself. Now I don't have any money left to hire any help. I keep a good garden and folks around help me out from time to time with game they've killed, but it's so embarrassing to have to accept charity after being so well off all those years."

C.B. decided that losing her husband and falling on hard times had created in her a sympathy for his situation, and this was why she was being so generous and helpful to him. Later, though, he could have kicked himself because he should have seen the signs right away. This woman wanted more than just to be his nurse, and she had once been accustomed to getting whatever she wanted. That kind of woman is dangerous for this kind of man. A man who has to watch his back can't afford to be caught watching a woman. And a man who has to stay on the move can't afford to be drawn back to a place where his adversaries think he might want to be.

CHAPTER 6

On his third day at Lillian's ranch, C.B. heard horses approaching. He quickly glanced out the window to find what he feared. It was three men who had to be the remaining Longley brothers. Lillian told him to stay quiet and out of sight, and she would get rid of them. He strapped his guns on, though, just in case.

She went out onto the porch to greet the men. Sure enough, they asked about him. "Ma'am, have you seen a feller lately a-ridin' a big Appaloosa, dressed in black an' totin' two guns? He killed two of our brothers an' we're a-huntin' 'im. We tracked 'im in this direction, but we lost the trail a mile or so back."

"Yes, he came by a couple of days ago, but," she lied, "he left after getting a poultice and bandages for his wound. He looked to be in pretty bad shape and I told him there was a doctor in Reedsville. Maybe that's where he went. It's just a few miles further east."

One of the men said, "Well, we'll go on into town and look around. If he's still there, we'll find 'im. If he's left there, he won't be a-travellin' very fast. If he's in that bad a shape, maybe we got time to rest up some. There a hotel in town?"

"Yes, The Hamlin House, right in the middle of town."

"Well, if you see 'im or hear from 'im again, we'd be obliged if you'd git word to us there."

"I surely will!"

C.B. knew he needed to be making tracks away from Reedsville. His side was healing pretty good, and now that the Longley boys had caught up with him, he realized this was a good time to change his direction. "I'll be movin' on in the mornin', Ma'am. I'm grateful for everything you've done, but I need to put some distance between me an' them."

She said, "You need more rest. They won't be back. When they can't find you in town, they'll ride further on and it'll be safe for you to stay."

But he said, "No, it's best if I push on. I've got rested up a bit an', with them goin' east, I'll head north an' should be able to travel a little easier. There's a little town I know of, several miles north of here, Cedar Grove. If they keep goin' east, I should lose 'em an' I can rest some more there."

"You don't need to go," she protested. "You can stay here. I'll keep you hidden and you can help around the ranch. It could be a good ranch again if it was worked. It could make a good home for you. You wouldn't have to be on the run anymore."

"Ma'am," he insisted, "I'll be leavin' in the mornin'. I thank you for the offer, but I'll be on my way."

He was adamant, but she was, too. She had to find a way to make him stay. With her husband's death, the ranch run down and having to spend what money her husband had saved, she desperately needed a man around.

When she found him saddling his Appaloosa the next morning, she lost whatever semblance of civility she had left. She was tired of living hand-to-mouth, often depending on the charity of her neighbors, It was humiliating, especially when she had been accustomed to having money, living well, having the best of everything. She needed to regain her "rightful" position at the top of the local social ladder, and the best opportunity she had seen so far was getting ready to ride away.

"After all I've done for you," she said, "nursed your wound, fed you, hid you out, lied for you, you're just going to leave? You owe me more than that! Why, if it weren't for me, you'd be dead by now! You need to stay!"

At this point, he lost whatever respect he had left for her, and his gratitude for her compassion evaporated. He realized that her motive had nothing to do with compassion, only selfishness. "What I really need to do," he thought, "is to get away from you, an' the sooner, the better". He shook his head, mounted up and spurred the Appaloosa toward the north.

As he rode away, she knew what she would do. No one uses her like this! No one rejects her and gets away with it! No one! The nerve of such a man! She watched until he was out of sight, then hitched up her buggy and drove into Reedsville.

She went to the Hamlin House, where she knew the Longley brothers were staying. She slipped up the outside stairs and went directly to their room and knocked softly. When the door opened, she lied and said, "He came back. He left again, but I know where he's headed. There's a town called Cedar Grove..." Now she would make him regret leaving her. They let her in and, a short discussion later, the woman and the brothers were all wearing that vengeful smile that accompanies the anticipated defeat of an enemy.

CHAPTER 7

As he watched from the mouth of the cave, C.B. knew that the snowfall was making this mountain the best choice for a place to lay low. No one would think of looking for him here, even if they had been able to get up here through the snow. He had known of this cave for years, even used it a few times when he needed to.

There was plenty of room for him and the horse, and he had laid in a good stock of supplies and firewood. It would also give him a little extra time to heal. The wound was coming along just fine, but he was still a little weak and could use the rest. And you never could tell...when the Longley boys couldn't find him in Reedsville, they might circle back to Lillian's ranch, just in case he had come back. But he was hoping that, by the time the snow was gone, his adversaries would be gone too. A man could always hope.

It had been a long, cold week, but the snow was gone now, and it was time for him to push on to the next town. As he saddled the Appaloosa, he was thinking about the next town. There was always a "next town." Often, he yearned for a "next town" which would be the *last* town he would need...a town where he could settle down, where no one knew who or what he was or had been.

He figured his next stop would be Cedar Grove. It was a nice, quiet little town, some place he could be happy to settle down in. Would it be the "next town" he was looking for, or would there be another "Johnny Longley" there? Or would Johnny's brothers be there, waiting for him? There was no point in wondering. The answer could only be found by going.

He threw a leg over the saddle and urged the Palouse down the mountain.

As he rode into Cedar Grove, C.B.'s eyes scanned the town for signs of trouble. Longley boys or not, he had a habit of always watching for trouble. He liked Cedar Grove. He had been there several times without any incidents and, though the people there knew him somewhat, they didn't know anything of his past. They didn't know of the speed of his guns or how often they had been used; and when he rode through Cedar Grove, he always kept his second gun out of sight, to minimize concern by the townspeople. They seemed to like and respect this pleasant man who drifted by on occasion, who minded his own business and never caused any trouble. He was beginning to allow himself to hope that Cedar Grove could be the place where he could finally let his guns rest.

He swung down in front of The Aces Saloon, named for the poker hand that had won the place for its current owner. As he entered, he saw a smile growing on the bartender's face. "Howdy, C.B. How you been?"

"Good, Ed. How 'bout you?" It was nice to be welcomed into a place for a change. His pleasure turned to concern, though, when he saw the smile on Ed's face turn down and his eyes narrow. "What is it, Ed?"

Ed poured C.B. a drink. "You know I don't butt into nobody's business, an' I don't know what's a-goin' on, but I oughta tell ya, there's three men been in here askin' 'bout you, er somebody that fits your description. They never said what it was about, but they looked like trouble. They sure didn't look like the law, an' they been ridin' a long, dusty trail. You got some kinda trouble? It ain't none of my business, but if you need help, you could have it. There's prob'ly people in town that would side ya 'gainst them strangers if'n you need it."

C.B. took a long, deep breath, then let it out slowly. "Thanks Ed, but I need to handle this myself. There's already two men dead in this situation, just on account of rash judgment. If I can help it, I don't want nobody else gettin' hurt, 'specially not on my account. Tell me 'bout these men. What did they say?"

"Well, one of 'em did all the talkin'. First, he asked about a hotel, then about a place to eat. I told him 'bout the Cedar Grove Hotel an' Maryann's Rest'rant. Then he described somebody that sounded like you, but said he was totin' two guns. Didn't say why they was lookin', but said if anybody saw you, they'd be down at the hotel or at Maryann's place, an' fer somebody to let 'em know when you come into town...'*when*,' not '*if*.' They're expectin' ya."

Ed hesitated a moment, then added, "Also, I noticed when you come in, Tully Owens' eyes got big an' he took outta here like his tail was on fire. They prob'ly know you're here by now. Ol' Tully'd sell out his own ma fer a drink of whiskey. You want another drink?"

"No thanks Ed. I'll need a clear head, a clear eye an' sure hands for what's about to happen."

"You sure you don't want some help?"

"No, I'll take care of it. They been doggin' me for weeks. I been tryin' to avoid this, but it's time it was put to rest."

An old man C.B. new only as "Milt" had been standing at the bar listening to the conversation, and now slid closer to C.B. "Son, I've knowed a lotta men in my day, an' I kin purty well tell the bad 'ns from the good 'ns at first look. Them boys is bad 'ns. Longleys, ain't they? I thought I reco'nized 'em when they come in. I knowed their pa years back, rid with 'im a while. He was a right easy-goin' feller, maybe too easy; he spoilt them boys, let 'em have their way 'bout ever'thing, give 'em ever'thing... ever'thing, that is, 'cept the discipline they needed. Looks like they growed up a-thinkin' they could do whutever they want. They'll be the sneaky type. You said you don't want nobody a-he'pin' ya an' I respect that, but you better keep yer eyes an' ears open. A rattlesnake'll give ya warnin' 'fore he strikes; I don't figger these boys will. You jist watch yerself, son."

C.B. could see a real concern in the old man's eyes. "Thanks Milt." He turned and walked slowly to the door, where he stopped, took his belly gun out of its crossdraw holster under his coat, turned it around and put it in his belt, where he could more easily draw it with his left hand if necessary.

Behind him, Ed said worriedly to Milt, "Three ag'inst one. That ain't much of a fair fight."

But Milt had watched C.B. stop at the door, and recognized his motions for what they were. A knowing grin grew upon his face and he said, "Which d'rection ya mean, Ed?" and walked toward the door.

CHAPTER 8

C.B. stepped into the dusty street, knowing that the three men would undoubtedly be waiting toward the other end, waiting to avenge their brothers. Two of them were; they were just coming out of the hotel. Where was the other one? He'd have to be as careful as Milt had suggested. He heard the saloon doors swing open and looked quickly behind him to see Milt come out, step to the end of the porch next to the gap between the buildings, sit down in a chair and prop his feet up on a box. "Don't pay me no mind, son, I won't git in yer way. The *last* place I wanna be right now is in *yore* way!" C.B.'s instincts, and what he knew of Milt, told him he could trust this old man, so he didn't object to Milt's being there.

Down the street, the two Longleys looked up at C.B. as he walked slowly toward them, his hands hanging loosely at his sides. He looked like he didn't have a care in the world, but his every nerve was alive with anticipation, his muscles poised to strike at the first movement from the men.

The two brothers slowly spread apart in the street, but it wasn't wide enough to get them out of reach of his aim.

He spoke softly, just loud enough for them to hear. "There's no need for this. I tried to ignore Johnny, but he just wouldn't let it go. His ego got the best of him an' he drew. The other one fired first, too. Another minute an' I would have been gone, an' he would still be alive."

The oldest brother said, "Makes no differ'nce. They're dead an' you did it."

C.B. still hoped they would see the pointlessness of this whole thing. "Your pa has already lost two sons; don't make 'is grief any worse."

"He's beyond grief now. Losin' Johnny sent 'im to 'is grave. Now, we're gonna send you to yours."

The two Longleys drew as one, but only one even cleared leather before C.B.'s guns found their targets. That one's bullet went wide, but C.B.'s didn't.

Suddenly, another shot rang out behind C.B.! He whirled quickly to see Milt, still sitting in the chair, his feet still propped up; but now, there was a gun in his hand pointed toward the gap between the buildings, where the body of the third Longley lay still in the dust.

Milt stood up, looked at C.B. and quietly said, "Can't abide a back-shooter."

He headed back into the saloon and said, "You take care now son."

If anyone had been watching or listening closely, they would have seen C.B. slowly shake his head and softly say, "A waste." But they only saw him mount his Appaloosa and walk it slowly toward the trail...a trail to the "next town,"...maybe to the last town he would ever need? Well, a man could always hope.

EPILOGUE

It was hot. That brassy sun had scorched this wasteland for centuries, and again it was beginning to work on him.

And again he rode, under a burning sun, on a sagebrush trail to who-knows-where.

BOOK 3

AT TRAIL'S END

PROLOGUE

"Most legends never got to retire," Cody Hays said, as he continued his story. "Bill Hickok was shot at a gamblin' table, Bill Tilghman was killed by a crooked lawman. Oh, a few of 'em made it, but it was rare. Bat Masterson moved to New York to avoid getting' into more gunfights, Wyatt Earp went to Alaska where nobody knew 'im, Jeff Milton was born late enough to outlive the outlaws of the Old West.

"Mostly though, if a legend wanted to retire, he had to stop bein' a legend first. An' that's just what Colton Bonner was tryin' to do."

CHAPTER 1

The man who called himself simply "C.B." was on the run. Not from the law, though that's why many men in the nineteenth century American West changed their names and took to the trails. No, he was running from a legend, a reputation built by a man named Colton Bonner.

Over the last several years, Colton had made a name for himself as a range detective, as a lawman and as a gunman. The more he plied his trades, the more that name evolved into a reputation. Eventually, he was so well known and feared among outlaws, that several gangs even offered a bounty for his elimination. That was the deciding factor which forced him into a life of drifting; away from his enemies if possible, or away from the consequences of eliminating them if not.

The only way to survive seemed to be to stay anonymous. Ever since the bounty on him was issued, he had been using only his initials and had kept on the move. If anyone pressed him for a last name, he had randomly chosen "Hays." One name was as good as another. It wasn't much of a life, living in the elements most of the time, sleeping on the ground, eating camp food, but it kept him alive. He stopped in towns whenever he felt it was safe, getting a hotel room and eating in a restaurant. Sooner or later, though, he would run into an old adversary and have to defend himself, or someone would figure out who he was, or at least *what* he was. Either way, fight or not, the local peace officer would end up suggesting he move along.

Vanceburg had been one of those towns that was far enough out of the way not to present much of a risk to C.B., or so he thought. A small town, it had none of the things that would attract the attention of outlaws; no bank, no affluent businesses, no large ranches. C.B. rode in one evening and saw a hotel/saloon, which seemed to be the only hotel or saloon in town.

He tied his roan to the hitch rail, stepped up to the door and hesitated long enough to look for any familiar faces inside. Not seeing any, he walked to the bar and ordered a drink. Without seeming to, he surveyed the crowd to see if he was attracting any attention. No one was looking his way, so he relaxed just a little. When he finished his drink, he stepped over to the hotel desk and registered for a room. "Got a livery in town?" he asked the clerk.

"Blacksmith has a stable at the south end of the street," he replied. "You be stayin' long?"

"Day or two prob'ly. Been a long trail, hopin' to rest up a bit. Got a restaurant or cafe in town?"

"No," the clerk replied, "but we got a dinin' room through that door there. Food's good. Not fancy, but good."

"Thanks," C.B. said, and went out to see to his horse. After stabling the roan, he went back in to the dining room and had a simple but filling supper, then climbed the stairs to his room for a hopefully restful night.

C.B. took advantage of the opportunity to sleep in a bit the next morning. He didn't get up until about seven a.m., and had a leisurely breakfast of ham, eggs and pancakes. It was the first good breakfast he had eaten in over a week. Afterwards, he went to the stable and curried his roan. Although he didn't always have the opportunity, he did always try to take good care of the horses he had ridden. Out here, especially with the kind of life C.B. led, a man's life might depend on his horse. On foot in the middle of the wilderness, a man was at the mercy of the elements and predators, both animal and human. It could turn out to be fatal. That's why horse thieves were hanged; they were considered equal to murderers.

Later, back at the saloon, he got a beer, went to an empty table against the far wall and, as an excuse to be seen minding his own business, dealt himself a hand of solitaire. He was enjoying the peacefulness of the day, when he saw a badge come in the door. Knowing he had done nothing wrong was of no comfort; he could guess what was coming. The Town Marshal's eyes swept the room and came to rest on C.B. After a brief visual assessment, the Marshal came over, sat down across the table and introduced himself. "You gonna be in town long?" he asked.

"No, just passin' through, restin' up for a day or two."

After a short pause, the Marshal asked, "Should I know you?"

C.B. hesitated just a moment, then said, "I would prefer that you didn't." Seeing the concern on the Marshal's face, he continued, "Look, I'm not here to cause trouble. Trouble is the last thing I want. I'm not wanted for anything anywhere, I just want to rest a bit before gettin' back on the trail."

After some thought, the Marshal said, "We've got a peaceful little town here an' the people wanna keep it that way. The way we keep it peaceful is we're very careful about toleratin' strangers, especially drifters. Now, you might not want any trouble, but for all we know, trouble might be followin' you up the trail. The people in this town can't be sure of any of that, so maybe the best thing is for you not to stay too long. I'm not orderin' you to leave, but for all we know, tomorrow could turn out to be another story. You get the idea?"

"It's a familiar idea," C.B. said with a sigh. "I'll pull out in the mornin'"

The Marshal got up and gave C.B. one more good lookover. "I can't help but think I should know who you are. I don't feel too worried about you for some reason, but the town might be; an' if they are, it's my job to be worried for 'em. Understand?"

"Of course," C.B. said. "I've been there."

The Marshal's expression eased just a bit and he said, "Somehow, I felt like you had. Luck to ya."

"Well," C.B. thought, "that could've been a lot worse. I just wish it had been better. Maybe one day I'll find a town where it *will* be better." The next morning, he was on his roan headed down the south trail.

CHAPTER 2

C.B.'s encounter with Vanceburg had been better than with most towns. Flatwoods, Louisa, Radcliff; they all had someone, usually a youngster, trying to prove he was the bull of the woods. All it took was to see a stranger drift in wearing two guns and they were ready to throw out a challenge.

The only exception to the string of towns C.B. had to leave had been Cedar Grove. It was a quiet little town, well off the beaten path, quiet enough and small enough to have no Marshal to run him out of town. He had, by the time he first saw Cedar Grove, adopted the habit of keeping his second gun, the one in the crossdraw holster, hidden under his coat; available for quick access if necessary, but unavailable as a temptation to any reputation hunters he might encounter. Cedar Grove had shown no evidence of having any of these.

When C.B. had first arrived in Cedar Grove, his first stop, as in almost all towns, was the saloon. A saloon was the best place to make an initial assessment of a town

110

because men from every segment of its society could be found there at one time or another. In addition to being a place for entertainment and social gathering, the saloon was also a meeting place for businessmen to discuss their trade and to negotiate transactions. It was where a man could hear the latest news and learn about the town and its citizens. All a man had to do was keep his mouth shut and his ears open. C.B. was good at both of those.

That first evening, at the bar, C.B. had been trying to study the crowd without seeming to do so, and noticed an older man watching him. The old man was obviously not a young reputation hunter, but neither was he wearing a badge, at least not where it could be seen. C.B. decided to keep his eye on the old man, just in case.

After a while, the old man eased over to the bar beside C.B. "Howdy," was all he said at first.

"Howdy," C.B. replied and motioned for the bartender to pour the old man a drink.

"Obliged," the old man said. "Lookin' fer a job, er jist passin' through?"

"Just passin' through."

"Jist as well; no jobs ta be had 'round here. Name's Milt."

"C.B." They shook hands. "Seems like a nice town,"

"Real nice," Milt agreed. "Quiet, friendly. Suits us jist fine."

"I can appreciate that," C.B. said, looking Milt straight in the eye. "Quiet towns suit me, too. Hope to retire to one someday."

Milt studied C.B.'s face for a quick moment, then indicated a table over by the wall. "Set fer a minute?" he asked.

They moved to the table and Milt allowed C.B. to choose the chair that backed up to the wall. That didn't go unnoticed. It was also apparent to C.B. that he was still being studied. He grinned slightly and said, "Are you the welcoming committee?"

Milt returned his grin and said, "No, jist bein' friendly is all. Cain't hep bein' curious, though...like I said, a quiet town suits us jist fine."

"You got nothin' to worry about with me," C.B. said. "I meant it when I said it suits me, too."

"Whur ya from?"

"Oh, back that way."

"Whur ya headed?"

"Over that way. I just want a place to get out of the saddle for a little while, that's all. I'll be on my way soon enough."

Milt seemed to be satisfied with that. He suggested the Cedar Grove Hotel and Maryann's Restaurant, then the conversation turned to small talk and news from the trail.

At the end of the evening, Milt asked, "You be stayin' on fer awhile, then?"

C.B. was pleasantly surprised by the friendly tone of the question and said with a smile, "Only a day or two, I reckon."

"Well, if'n I don't see ya 'til then, stop in an' say g'bye 'fore ya leave."

Put at ease, at least as much as was possible for him, by the encounter with the man called Milt, C.B. checked into the Cedar Grove Hotel for the best night's sleep he'd had in quite a while. The next morning, he found out just how good a cook Maryann was, and made a point to tell her so. Maybe now he had two friends in town.

He went to the stable and curried the Appaloosa he was riding these days, the best trail horse he had ever owned, then spent the rest of the morning in the hotel lobby, reading the back issues of newspapers sent in from a number of cities across the country. After lunch, he made good use of one of the chairs on the porch of the saloon, and the afternoon sunshine that went with it.

After supper, he went back to the saloon for a last drink and saw Milt at the bar. After a little talk about how well he had been able to relax here in Cedar Grove, C.B. told Milt he would be leaving the next morning. "So soon?" Milt asked.

"Yeah, I don't want to wear out my welcome, especially in a town as nice as this one. I'd like to be able to come back some day."

"Well, I ain't heard no one complainin'. I reckon you'll be welcome ta come back."

As C.B. rode out the next morning, he couldn't stop thinking about how nice it had been to be somewhere he could relax. He was afraid of pushing his luck, but he certainly would come back to Cedar Grove when he got the chance, and when he felt it was safe. As it turned out, he had several chances from time to time, and took advantage of them.

He became familiar with several of the faces, and got to know a few of the people in town; not well, but enough to speak to. He never discussed himself with them however, at least not in any detail. He was as friendly to everyone as he could afford to be, but he didn't want to drag anyone into the life he was trying to stay ahead of.

Things had gone well with Cedar Grove up until that business with the Longley brothers. C.B. had been passing through Mill Creek one day and had been braced in the saloon by the youngest brother. C.B. had to kill him in self-defense and when the other four brothers heard about it, they came looking for him.

C.B. had gone to Old Mexico to wait for things to cool down, but when he came back, they were still on his trail. One of them cornered him in a stable and C.B. had to eliminate him, which just made the other three more determined than ever to track him down.

He thought he had given them the slip at one point, and figured it was safe enough to hole up in the only place he thought he wouldn't be asked to leave. But his destination had been betrayed, and the Longleys had come to Cedar Grove to ambush him. He managed to get two of them and, as the last one was sneaking up behind him to shoot him in the back, old Milt had come to his aid and eliminated that one.

This, C.B. figured, would ruin Cedar Grove for him now. He rode out of town, saddened by the fact that he had been the cause of trouble in this nice little town, and that he probably would no longer be welcome in it.

CHAPTER 3

Two things C.B. realized after the incident in Cedar Grove with the Longley brothers: living constantly on the move was not going to keep his old life at bay, and his desire for a stable home and family was growing stronger every day. This made Cedar Grove all the more attractive to him, but he was reluctant to press his luck with its townspeople.

After considerably more time riding the trails, it finally became more than C.B. could ignore. He determined to return to Cedar Grove and test the waters. At worst, they would tell him to keep moving, which he was already doing anyway. He hoped, however, that they would at least tolerate him enough to allow him to settle on a ranch somewhere outside of town.

As usual, once he had made up his mind, C.B. was eager to get on with it. He turned his Paloose and headed in the direction of Cedar Grove.

The morning was quiet as C.B. rode into Cedar Grove. He had decided that his best bet would be to talk to Milt. Milt would be likely to know the attitude of the town and would be honest but friendly with him. He thought he might find Milt at Maryann's Restaurant this time of morning, so he made that his first stop.

He found Milt sitting at a table in the corner. As he approached, Milt looked up and smiled, which relieved C.B. more than he would have expected. "Glad ta see ya, son," Milt said.

"An' I'm glad to hear you say that."

"Why's that?" Milt asked.

"After what happened the last time I was here, I didn't know whether I would be welcome in town."

"Son, these folks surely do love their quiet little town, but they ain't blind and they ain't unrealistic. An' it ain't like this town ain't never seen no trouble afore. The reason Cedar Grove is so quiet is 'cause in the rare case when trouble did come, it was put a stop to quick.

"These folks all seen them Longley boys, an' they all knowed you didn't have no choice in the matter. It wan't yore fault; they didn't give ya no other way out. Fact is, there was a bit o' talk after you left 'bout whuther you'd come back er not. Opinion was, it'd be a good thing ta have a quiet, friendly man like y'self aroun', who's able ta stop somethin' afore it gits too fur outta hand."

"But aren't they afraid I would turn out to be too violent?" C.B. asked.

"Son, I been around a long time. I'm a purty good judge o' men. I kin read men better'n most folks kin read a book. Y'know, a man kin be judged by the enemies he makes, an' we all seen three of the enemies you've made. Now, I might not know 'xactly *who* you are (I got my suspicions, mind ya), but I figger I know *what* you are; an' I wouldn't mind seein' ya stick around."

The remark about who he was worried C.B. a little, and it must have shown on his face, because Milt was quick to say, "Now, don't you worry none, boy, I ain't said nothin' ta nobody. I figgered if'n you hadn't said nothin', I wan't a-goin' to, neither. Yore life is yore business. But I know enough to figger we'd likely do well ta try ta keep ya 'round."

"What makes you think you might know who I am?" C.B. asked. His biggest worry was that his enemies would know of his whereabouts.

"You ain't never asked me whut my last name was, have ya?" said Milt, keeping his voice low. "It's Jefferson. Ever hear that name?"

Milt Jefferson! One of the most capable and respected lawmen C.B. had ever heard of...Texas Ranger, U.S. Marshal. When he got on your trail, you were as good as caught. No wonder he suspected who C.B. was. "This must be a safe place to retire to," said C.B. "Do the folks here know?"

"A few, but they don't talk about it. I got my enemies, too. By the way, if'n you *do* stick around, we'll need ta know whut last name yore a-usin'."

"It's Hays," he said. "If I *did* settle here, I'd have to work out some details first: find a place, maybe start a ranch, that kind of thing."

Suddenly, their conversation was interrupted, when a man came rushing in, out of breath. "Milt! Arlen Miller was just robbed and shot! His two ranch hands held him up for the money from his last cattle drive and, when he tried to stop them, they shot him several times, then took out on two of his best horses. Doc patched him up best he could; he's still alive, but it doesn't look good."

Milt jumped up. "Go git Frank Webb an' Charlie Mallory an' tell 'em ta saddle their best trail horses an' meet me here in thirty minutes." He looked toward the kitchen and saw Maryann standing in the door. "Maryann, put together grub fer four

119

men fer four days." He looked at C.B. "Go with us?" It was more a directive than a request.

It didn't take much persuasion; C.B.'s instincts, and his feelings for this community, already had him rising to his feet.

CHAPTER 4

Their first step was to ride to Arlen Miller's ranch to pick up the trail of the two robbers. Milt checked the corral and noticed the absence of Arlen's gray gelding and his pinto mare. They would know the track of the gray because it had one barred shoe and they would be able to study the track of the accompanying pinto on the way.

At first, the trail was easy to follow, because the two men were in a hurry to get away and didn't take time to hide their trail. As they went, however, they began to take more care in choosing their path so as to take advantage of rocks and hard ground. Milt wanted C.B. to ride in front with him because he was sure C.B. would prove to be a good tracker. He was right.

The further they went, the slower they had to go, due to the increased efforts of the two fugitives to hide their trail. At one point, they crossed a stream and, as suspected, the two men didn't emerge directly across from their point of entry. Frank and Charlie stopped in the stream while Milt went upstream and C.B. went downstream.

121

Most fugitives believe that running water will hide their trail, and with the average tracker, that might be true; but when a tracker had as much experience as Milt and C.B. had, he knew what to look for. C.B. found it about fifty yards downstream. He called to the other men and, when they reached him, he pointed to a rock in the stream that had a small fresh nick in it where a horseshoe had scuffed it.

"They came this way, all right," he said. Frank and Charlie looked at each other in amazement. They knew they would never have found that nick. "You boys look for tracks on both banks where they would've come out. I'll keep lookin' for sign in the stream."

They went another quarter of a mile or so, until Milt said, "Here! They come out on these rocks." They continued following the trail over various terrain, sometimes with ground so hard, the only way to track them was by spotting a broken twig or even a horse's hair stuck on a briar. Because they knew the colors of the horses they were following, it wasn't too difficult to confirm they were on the right track.

Occasionally, they would lose the trail altogether and would have to spread out and ride in ever-increasing circles until they picked up new sign. Other men might have gotten discouraged by this time, but Milt and C.B. were used to tracking for days on end and, if the other two weren't, they were driven by their desire for justice for their friend and by their determination to deal decisively with people who would do harm to their community and their friends.

By the end of their second day out, they noticed a slight change in the trail. The fugitives were not being quite as careful as they had been. Either they were getting tired, or they thought any possible pursuers would have lost the trail, or even given up by now. Far from giving up, their pursuers were rejuvenated by it.

The morning of the third day, they came upon what was apparently the fugitives' camp from the night before. The rocks around the fire were still slightly warm, so they couldn't have departed much more than a couple of hours ago. Frank and Charlie wanted to hurry on, but C.B. and Milt wanted to take just a few minutes to look around the camp first.

"Two men," C.B. said, "one wearin' old fashioned boots with mule-ear straps, carryin' his gun crossdraw. Thought for a minute he was left-handed, but some of his cigarettes and matches didn't make it all the way to the fire. They were tossed by his right hand."

"That'll be Harlan," said Milt. "This was them, alright."

"How could you tell about the holster and boots?" Charlie asked.

"Marks in the dirt where he sat," said C.B. "A little mark either side of each boot made by the straps hangin' down an' a mark on his left side where the toe of his holster hung down. No holster marks on his right side."

Milt smiled and thought to himself, "Yep. He'd be a good 'n to have around."

They mounted and continued the journey, able to travel a little faster, now that the fugitives weren't being as careful. It shouldn't be long until they overtook their quarry. In fact, it was only about three hours later that they found them.

CHAPTER 5

As the small posse rode into the little town of Grayson, they realized things would be more complicated here than out on the trail. On the trail, there would be no innocent bystanders to watch out for, no women or children to be endangered by flying bullets, if it came to that; and with people who would shoot a man multiple times for money, it usually came to that. If they were to take these men in town, they would need to do some planning first.

The first thing was to try to locate their quarry without being seen themselves. This turned out to be the easy part; a gray gelding and a pinto mare were standing at the hitch rail in front of a saloon. There was no way to know how many people were in the saloon, so the safe thing would be to try to get the two men outside, where they could be surrounded and taken quickly.

"The first thing is to tie their horses hard and fast," C.B. said, "so they can't get away quick if they come out. They're no doubt just hitched with a slip knot. Frank, you an' Charlie stay outside. Find a place to

125

stand where you can get a good angle on 'em if we can get 'em outside. I'll go in first. They don't know me, an' I should be able to get to the other side of the room without 'em gettin' the wind up."

Milt said, "I'll come in a minute later. They know me, so they'll know right off why I'm there. I'll circle 'em opposite to you, C.B., then we'll let 'em know you're after 'em, too. Hopefully, that'll make 'em head fer the door. If'n they do, we'll have 'em. If'n they don't, we'll jist hafta take 'em best we kin inside." Turning to Frank and Charlie, he said, "If'n you hear shootin' an' they come a-runnin' out, you boys nail 'em. Don't wait fer us, don't try ta take 'em alive. If they shoot their way out, they're too dangerous ta let go; jist' nail 'em. Got it?"

Frank and Charlie both agreed they had no problem at all with following those instructions. They took their rifles and headed for positions across the street where they had clear shots at the saloon door and the hitch rail.

C.B. walked slowly into the saloon as if he were just coming in for a drink. He quickly recognized the two men from the descriptions Milt had given him. He noticed the mule-ear boots and the crossdraw holster. They were standing at about the middle of the bar, so C.B. headed toward the right end and ordered a drink. About that time, Milt came in and went to the left. The two men noticed him immediately and turned to face him. They knew at once they had a problem, they just didn't know how big a problem until they heard C.B. behind them say, "You boys are under arrest."

They froze, but the rest of the room moved quickly. The two looked at each other and realized they had to make a quick choice. If they had been more experienced as criminals, they may have chosen a safer course of action. As it was, they made the more dangerous choice. Rather than be taken back to face a hanging, they thought that, since it was two against two, they should try to shoot their way out of this situation. That was the wrong choice.

Before C.B. had even spoken, he had his hand on his gun, and Milt grabbed his as soon as he saw the expressions on the two outlaws' faces. He had seen that expression so many times before and knew quite well what was coming next. The two former lawmen had been in this spot often enough that they didn't even think; their muscles simply reacted. It was no contest.

When the smoke cleared, C.B. went to the door and called for Frank and Charlie to give them a hand. They dragged the outlaws' bodies out, tied them across their horses and headed home.

CHAPTER 6

Back in Cedar Grove, the posse dropped the bodies off at the undertaker's, then Milt and C.B. headed to Arlen Miller's ranch to return his money and horses. Arlen was not only still alive, he was well enough to talk to them. He listened to their recounting of the adventure and, needless to say, he was grateful to the posse for recovering his money. Otherwise, he would have been broke and forced to sell his ranch.

"You boys don't know how grateful I am. Without that money, I'd be finished. I wanna give y'all a re-ward fer gittin' it back fer me."

"Nosir," Milt said. "Arlen, I won't take nothin' fer he'pin' a neighbor. You'd do the same fer me if'n it was th' other way 'round. I'm sure Charlie an' Frank feel the same way. You might be able ta do somethin' fer C.B., though. He might be willin' ta settle down in Cedar Grove if'n he had a job here." This was a surprise to C.B., but a welcome one.

Arlen's eyes brightened up a bit and he said, "I gotta have some he'p anyways,

128

'specially while I'm laid up a-healin'. C.B., we need a man like you 'round here. *I* need a man like you 'round here. Tell ya whut I'll do; if'n you hadn't got my money back, I wouldn't even have a ranch, so I owe you. How 'bout a partnership, fifty/fifty?"

"I couldn't take half your ranch, Mr. Miller," C.B. said.

"Sure you could! I'd still have half," Arlen said, "an' without you, I wouldn't have nothin'. Shucks, I really owe y'all the whole thing, but I know the others won't take nuthin', so it's up ta you! 'Sides, you'd work harder workin' fer yerse'f than fer someone else inyway. It's a bargain fer me. 'Sides, I ain't got no one ta pass it on to, noways. You might as well be the one ta git it when I'm gone."

"Take it, boy!" Milt interjected. "We need you 'round here!"

This would be the chance to settle down that C.B. had been longing for! His mind raced quickly southward, to the little Mexican town of Poca and a girl named Elena, who was waiting for him there. It was almost too much for him to absorb. "If you're serious about this," he said, "I'd like nothin' better than to take you up on it."

"I'm as serious as I ever been. I need he'p bad, an' I owe you a lot."

"Well then, I'll take it. There's one thing, though. If I'm gonna settle down here,

I need to make a trip down to Old Mexico soon as I can. There's a girl down there..."

"Say no more," Milt grinned. "How long'll ya hafta be gone?"

"Maybe a couple of weeks."

"Kin ya go soon?"

"The sooner the better."

"You go on, then. I'll stay with Arlen 'til you git back. I ain't as able as I used ta be, but I kin watch a few cows fer a couple weeks, I reckon. I ain't got much else ta do, noways."

"I'll leave in the mornin'"

"You don't wanna rest up a couple days fust?"

"No, sir! I don't wanta waste a day."

On the trail to Mexico, C.B. worked hard to convince himself this was really happening. For years, he had longed for a place to settle down, raise a family and own a ranch, somewhere his adversaries wouldn't look for him, somewhere his friends would keep his secret and where he could live in obscurity. Cedar Grove seemed to be just that place, a place where he could hide from his own legend. Now, maybe he would finally be able to put his old life behind him, marry Elena, raise strong sons and leave them a legacy they could be proud of.

As the years went by, either his enemies couldn't find him, forgot about him or were killed or captured by other lawmen. C.B. Hays lived out his days peacefully, as a rancher and family man, and the legend of Colton Bonner was finally put to rest.

EPILOGUE

C.B. Hays died of natural causes in 1924 at the age of 72. His friends and neighbors who had gathered around the grave site were surprised to see the name "Colton Bonner" on his headstone. He had wanted to be buried under his birth name and, until the day of his funeral, only his family knew.

Old Milt had been the only one who had realized who he was, but a couple of the old timers recognized the name. One said, "Well, I'll be!" Another nodded and said, "Reckon I coulda guessed." The rest were too young to know anything about his legend, and that would have suited Colton nicely.

As for me, I consider myself fortunate to have heard the legend of Colton Bonner from the man who, as a young boy, heard the story at Colton's own knee...Colton's grandson, Cody Bonner Hays.